Tempting the Scoundrel

Book V of
The Seven Curses of
London

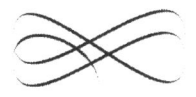

Lana Williams

Copyright © 2017 by Lana Williams
All rights reserved.

ISBN-13: 978-1976011276
ISBN-10: 1976011272

By payment of required fees, you have been granted the *non*-exclusive, *non*-transferable right to access and read the text of this book. No part of this text may be reproduced, transmitted, downloaded, decompiled, reverse engineered, or stored in or introduced into any information storage and retrieval system, in any form or by any means, whether electronic or mechanical, now known or hereinafter invented without the express written permission of copyright owner.

Please Note
The reverse engineering, uploading, and/or distributing of this book via the internet or via any other means without the permission of the copyright owner is illegal and punishable by law. Please purchase only authorized electronic editions, and do not participate in or encourage electronic piracy of copyrighted materials. Your support of the author's rights is appreciated

No part of this book may be reproduced or transmitted in any form or by any electronic or mechanical means, including photocopying, recording or by any information storage and retrieval system, without the written permission of the publisher, except where permitted by law.
Thank you.

Cover art by The Killion Group
http://thekilliongroupinc.com

Other Books in The Seven Curses of London series:

TRUSTING THE WOLFE, a novella, Book .5
LOVING THE HAWKE, Book 1
CHARMING THE SCHOLAR, Book 2
RESCUING THE EARL, Book 3
DANCING UNDER THE MISTLETOE, Book 4, a Christmas Novella
FALLING FOR THE VISCOUNT, Book 6, Coming Fall 2017

Want to make sure you know when my next book is released? Sign up for my newsletter at http://lanawilliams.net/.

Chapter One

London, England, April 1871

Elliott Walker, the Earl of Aberland, gave a sigh of relief as the hansom cab drew to a halt before his Mayfair residence. He paused after alighting, his gaze taking in the impressive entrance with its white fluted pillars and marble steps that he was fortunate enough to call home.

Each trip abroad made him more grateful to return to the peace he found within its walls. His secret position with the British Intelligence Office forced him to travel far more than he preferred.

This last visit to the Continent had been especially trying, causing him to question how much longer he wanted to continue. Playing the role of scoundrel to gather intelligence had become exhausting, and he was weary to the bone.

For the moment, he intended to put all his questions and doubts aside and enjoy time at home. The house was filled with pleasant memories, but even better, his beloved grandmother resided here. He smiled in anticipation of seeing her.

The door opened and two liveried footmen hurried

out, greeting him with a bow before tending to his bags.

Codwell, his longtime butler, waited by the door, smiling broadly as Elliott walked up the steps. "Welcome home, my lord."

"Thank you, Codwell. I trust all has been well in my absence?"

"Indeed."

If it weren't for his special training and natural instincts, Elliott might have missed the hesitancy in Codwell's manner. His thoughts flew to his grandmother. "Is all well with the countess?"

"Yes. She is most anxious to see you."

Guilt speared through Elliott. He'd been gone nearly four weeks, leaving his grandmother alone. He had the utmost faith in Codwell and the rest of the staff to keep watch over her safety, but she needed more than that. "I hope she's enjoying the beginning of the Season."

"Actually, I'd venture to say she's reveling in it."

"Oh?" Elliott stepped into the foyer, glancing about as though he might spot what caused his unease. Codwell's words sank in, returning his focus to the older man who'd been with his family since he was a young boy. "Reveling, you say?"

That wasn't like his grandmother. While she normally enjoyed attending a few events, he wouldn't have described her participation in previous years as "reveling."

The butler cleared his throat, shifting away his gaze briefly. "We have a new addition to the household."

"Who would that be?" Anger slid into Elliott, tightening his chest. Codwell knew a few details of Elliott's double life, so he understood why this news would not be welcome.

"With your long absence, your uncle feared the countess might be lonely, so he hired a companion for her, a Miss Sophia Markham."

The footmen entered with his bags, forcing Elliott to wait to have his questions answered. And he had many.

While he detested the idea of his grandmother being lonely, he equally detested the idea of a stranger living in his house.

He imagined a nosy, elderly spinster who refused to mind her own business. The idea of the sanctuary of his home breached by a stranger was impossible. He took care to hide his activities from the staff, with the exception of the butler and his grandmother, but he had no desire to evade another set of watchful eyes.

No. It simply wasn't bearable.

The butler turned to direct the footmen to take care with his belongings, and Elliott opened the door of his library only to stop short, startled to find a woman there, perusing the bookshelves. *His* bookshelves.

As though feeling the weight of his regard, the young lady turned to face him, her eyes widening in surprise. Lovely hazel eyes set in an attractive face. But none of that mattered. She was in *his* library, the one place he depended on as his refuge.

"My lord, may I introduce Miss Sophia Markham, your grandmother's new companion?" Codwell asked.

No, you may not. He bit his tongue to keep the words from slipping out, yet he saw nothing but complications when he looked at this woman.

Where was the elderly spinster who would be better suited for his grandmother? This young lady was the very opposite of what he'd expected. Dark curls framed her face, as though refusing to be tamed. Her alabaster skin begged to be touched, and one dark brow rose, as if already questioning him.

"Good day." He knew his tone was churlish and less than polite but couldn't seem to help himself.

She opened her mouth to respond then quickly closed it, instead dipping into a low curtsy. "My lord."

The surprise in her expression at his presence gave him a small measure of satisfaction. Perhaps he wasn't the only one feeling off balance.

He scowled. Why did she have to be so lovely? He would've much preferred the aging spinster he'd imagined.

She rose from her graceful curtsy in her plain grey gown and clasped her hands before her. "I'm terribly sorry to intrude in your library." Did she have the ability to read minds? "I was searching for a new book to read to the countess."

A likely story. His gaze swung toward his desk. But of course the polished mahogany was empty except for his grandfather's gold clock on its gleaming surface. He hadn't left any clues for an inquisitive guest to find, nor had any arrived in his absence.

The idea of having to guard against a nosy stranger who made herself at home in his library made him even wearier. He couldn't do it. Not only did his grandmother reside in his house, he spent a significant amount of time with her when he was home. That meant he'd be in contact with this young lady frequently. Far too frequently.

But before he did anything rash, such as send her packing, he would speak with his grandmother. If this woman was here at his uncle's behest, surely his grandmother wouldn't miss her company. Elliott would be rid of her in no time.

"I hope you found something of interest," he said at last.

She turned to pluck a slim leather-bound volume from a shelf. "This will do until the books we ordered arrive."

"What books would those be?" He was curious as to what his grandmother had been up to in his absence.

"*The Mystery of Edwin Drood* by Charles Dickens and *The Seven Curses of London* by James Greenwood." She lifted her chin, as though expecting him to question the choices. "Have you read either?"

"I can't say I have. *The Seven Curses?*"

"I understand the author shares the seven worst problems plaguing the city."

While his grandmother often read fiction, since when

had she become interested in social issues? He'd obviously been gone far too long.

Miss Markham pursed her lips. "Perhaps you might enjoy learning more about such problems."

He sighed at the hint of disapproval in her expression. His reputation had preceded him. While he knew he should be pleased his cover as a philandering rogue was secure, he'd grown weary of it.

"I shall rely on your report of it." He gave his signature careless smile as he moved closer, which only had her tightening her lips further.

Her unfavorable opinion of him could prove useful. Perhaps getting rid of her would be easier than he expected.

⋈

Sophia hardly knew what to think, and she certainly didn't know what to say. She felt as though she'd been caught rifling through the earl's personal things from the accusing way he stared at her.

The only reason she'd taken the position of companion to the Countess of Aberland was because the earl was rarely home. And because she liked her ladyship—adored her, actually. Though occasionally gruff, the woman had a kind heart, a keen intelligence, and a no-nonsense manner Sophia admired.

The earl was a different kettle of fish altogether. The date of his return had been uncertain, but it wasn't *today*. She hadn't had the proper time to prepare herself to meet the notorious scoundrel.

Her cousin, Dalia Fairchild, had warned her of the earl's reputation as a rogue, far more interested in chasing ladies on foreign shores than here in London. What she hadn't mentioned was how handsome he was.

He shared his grandmother's unique green eyes, the shade reminding her of a jade Buddha she'd seen in a museum when she was a child. They glowed with an internal light that made one look twice. Dark hair swept across his brow, and even darker brows arched over those intense eyes. His strong jawline with a hint of shadow from his beard caused the oddest sensation in her stomach, almost making her breathless.

Or perhaps that was caused by the way he stared at her, as though she were a puzzle he had yet to solve.

But that was nonsense. She was an open book with no secrets to hide. Besides, she held doubts he'd read a book since his university days. Scoundrels didn't often read, did they? In truth, she'd never before met one. Her father, who died when she was only six years, didn't count. She barely remembered him.

With a firm reprimand, she brought her thoughts back to the task at hand. She'd promised herself that when she met the earl, she would make it clear she was no one with whom to be trifled and he should set his roguish sights elsewhere. Not that a woman such as herself, raised in the country, headed for spinsterhood and dressed in half-mourning, would be to his tastes, but Aunt Margaret always told her that opportunity created desire.

"I'm terribly sorry to be in your way." She glanced at Codwell who remained by the door, hoping he'd help with this uncomfortable situation. If she wasn't mistaken, amusement twinkled in the butler's blue eyes. Assistance wouldn't be coming from that quarter.

"I am pleased we had a chance to meet before you leave." The earl stepped closer, causing her to shift back, only to bump against the shelves.

"Leave?" She could only blink at him, confused.

"Now that I've returned, your services will no longer be needed."

Panic skittered down her spine. "But I've only recently started in the position."

He gave a nod. "Then it should be easy for you to find another."

She knew her mouth opened and closed like a cod tossed on the river bank, gasping for air, but she couldn't help it. "I hope the countess will still be in need of my company."

"We shall see, but I'd suggest you pack your bags, just in case."

While she'd wondered if the earl would be displeased to find her in his household upon his return, she'd never expected to be dismissed on the spot.

"If you'll excuse me, I'm going to visit with my grandmother. Perhaps you'd like to remain in your room for a time."

She swallowed hard, heat filling her cheeks at his dismissal. She hadn't felt like a servant here until this moment. The countess had treated her with respect and kindness, quite the opposite of her grandson.

Yet she was well aware there was nothing she could do if he chose to let her go.

"Of course." She curtsied again, her mind blank with shock as she walked from the room, head held high with the book in her hand.

Keeping the outward signs of her worry at bay until she reached her room on the third floor was no easy task. Only once she closed her door behind her did she allow her shoulders to sag and her hands to tremble. She eased into the chair at her desk.

Just when she'd become accustomed to her new position, the earl had returned to threaten her carefully built world.

Sophia had feared what the future might bring when Aunt Margaret passed away unexpectedly six months ago, but then a timely letter from her cousin Dalia had arrived.

They'd met on one of Sophia's infrequent trips to London when her mother still lived. She and Dalia exchanged letters several times a year since their meeting, and Sophia always looked forward to them.

Sophia's life had changed drastically upon her father's

death, when she and her mother had gone to live with her aunt. Though a viscount, he'd spent his modest inheritance and her mother's dowry shortly after their marriage. Aunt Margaret had declared him a carousing rogue, but Sophia's mother loved him all the same, even after he'd left them penniless and in dire straits with his death.

Aunt Margaret had taken them in, but Sophia's mother succumbed to illness within two years of her husband's passing. Sophia had been devastated and still missed her.

Though grateful for Aunt Margaret, life hadn't been easy with her. Money was tight, and her aunt didn't believe in wasting time focusing on happiness. Sophia emerged from those years well educated and bearing a healthy dose of common sense and caution.

A letter from Dalia arrived at an opportune time, shortly after her aunt's funeral. When she'd shared news of her aunt's passing, Dalia responded immediately, telling her that her mother and father would be happy to provide her with a Season.

Sophia appreciated the offer, but after watching her mother's heartbreak and listening to her aunt's many lectures on the subject of men, Sophia had no desire to marry. But what choices did that leave her?

After several more letters, Dalia mentioned the possibility of serving as a companion. That seemed like the perfect solution to Sophia.

The Fairchilds had been kind enough to suggest she stay with them while she searched for a position. Sophia considered it luck that the countess, with whom the Fairchilds were acquainted, needed someone shortly after Sophia's arrival in London.

Her interview with the countess had gone well, and Sophia had been excited at the prospect of the position.

But now...she feared she was being abandoned to fate once again.

With a shaky sigh, she gathered her wits. The countess had never indicated that Sophia wouldn't be needed upon the earl's return. Surely, she would've mentioned such an important detail when she offered Sophia the position.

Maybe there was still hope.

But she had no doubt the earl would continue to be a problem. How could she convince him the countess needed her? There had to be something she could do. She feared she'd allowed her natural distaste for a man such as him to show. He represented everything she had been warned against most of her life.

Now she was in the uncomfortable circumstance of needing to not only hide her disapproval but gain his support if she wanted to remain in the position.

But how?

Chapter Two

Elliott knocked on his grandmother's withdrawing room door on the second floor. Not waiting for a response, he strode in, anxious to see her. He couldn't help but worry she was failing if his uncle had determined she needed a companion.

"Darling, we weren't expecting you." The Countess of Aberland's green eyes lit at the sight of him. "I'm thrilled you have returned at last." She gracefully rose from her favorite chair by the fire to greet him, arms outstretched, her smile as bright as the sun.

He realized he needn't have worried.

A flood of emotion coursed through him as he kissed her soft cheeks then gently embraced her, her lilac fragrance filling his senses. She and his grandfather had been his rock after his parents were killed when he was ten years. They had taken him in, offering comfort and familiarity to a lonely boy. Their love and support meant the world to him.

When his grandfather passed away five years ago, Elliott and his grandmother had grown even closer.

He eased back, his hands on her arms as he studied her beaming face. "You are as beautiful as ever."

She chuckled. "You sound just like your grandfather."

"The truth cannot be ignored." Few knew her true age of seventy-six years as her slim figure and good bone structure served her well. Her golden hair had faded to grey at the temples years ago, giving her a regal look. Bright green eyes sparkled with a joy for life that few matched.

She examined his appearance just as closely. "Judging by the shadows under your eyes, you've had too little rest. It's past time you returned home."

He dropped his gaze, not wanting her to see too much. His last mission had been exhausting. Living a double life meant few hours of sleep. He'd played the rogue in Paris, making certain he was seen at notable parties as well as at the more popular gaming hells and a brothel or two.

After the parties ended as well as during the day, he met with counterparts in French and Spanish Intelligence to compare notes and share fragments of the information he'd learned. Sharing more would have been foolhardy.

Intelligence work was much like a card game, where intentions and knowledge were kept close to the vest. His instincts for knowing whom he could trust gave him an advantage few others held. He liked to think he had his grandfather to thank for the skill.

The rumors of Prussia's growing power and alliances with Russia and Austria were of grave concern, especially to France. Any unrest on the Continent had direct ramifications to England, hence Elliott's visit.

He wondered how much his grandmother knew of his true activities. After all, he'd followed in his grandfather's footsteps by serving his country. As the wife of a lord involved in such an endeavor, she must have had her suspicions as to what her husband was up to, especially since the couple had shared a deep love—although only after being forced to marry to save her from ruin. His grandmother insisted that fate had intervened and one unexpected evening had changed everything for them.

"I'm pleased to be home at last," he answered. It didn't truly matter what she knew as he could never confirm nor deny his activities.

In his heart, he hoped she knew he was more than a scoundrel searching for the next good time and a new lover.

The question of who he was without his position in the Intelligence Office or his cover as a rogue was one that had bothered him of late. He'd been living a lie for so long, he was no longer sure who he truly was.

"Sit and tell me of your travels," she said as she released him.

He closed his eyes for a moment, almost wishing she hadn't asked. He hated to lie. Yet as he sifted through his memories of the past few weeks, he found a few truthful details he could share.

She'd travelled often with his grandfather and enjoyed hearing of the places she'd seen firsthand.

"If only you would agree to come with me on my next trip," he added after they had spoken for a time, knowing she would refuse just like she always did.

"Perhaps one of these days I will surprise you and do just that."

His stomach tightened at the thought. Did her sudden change of heart have something to do with the woman he'd found in his library? What sort of influence did she have over his grandmother?

"Now tell me of you. How have you fared?" He leaned back in his chair, pleased to be in her company but determined to discover what exactly had happened in his absence.

"I have news to share." Her eyes sparkled with joy. "I cannot wait for you to meet Sophia."

The image of the lady in question filled his mind. "I already have."

"Excellent. I know you'll adore her as much as I do. How I've managed all this time without her is a mystery.

When your Uncle Daniel suggested I have a companion, I thought it a terrible idea." She shook her head. "Why would I want someone underfoot all the time?"

Elliott clenched his jaw. That was exactly how he felt. Hopefully his grandmother would see why the woman could leave now that he'd returned.

"But Sophia is an absolute delight." Elliott's hopes were dashed by her words. "She is well-educated and clever and so eager to share new experiences."

"Humph." Those qualities did not suit him. Not when he was hiding his work as a spy.

"I confess I was feeling a bit blue and venturing out less and less during your absence."

Guilt reared its ugly head at her words. He'd been gone longer than he'd anticipated due to information he'd learned. Each rumor required careful study to sift through the lies to discover the truth. Given the alarming content, he'd stayed nearly ten days longer than he intended.

"My apologies for my lengthy absence." He bit his tongue before he confessed the reason for it.

"Oh, please." She waved a hand in dismissal of his words. "You have better things to do than keep an old woman company."

He started to reply only to realize any response would reveal things he shouldn't. At last he latched onto the truth he could share. "You know you are the love of my life."

She laughed, just as he hoped she would. Then she leaned forward as though to share a delicious secret. "I am most anxious for the day when you truly find the love of your life. I know your choice won't disappoint me."

His chest tightened at her words. The chances of that happening were nonexistent. If he were to follow in his grandparents' footsteps and find a great love, the woman would be falling for someone who didn't exist. He lived his life immersed in falsehoods. That wouldn't be true love.

"How could I possibly love anyone more than you?" he asked with a smile. Her laughter brushed away his worry.

"Whatever am I to do with you, Elliott? You are a scoundrel just like your grandfather." She sighed, her gaze focused on something only she could see. She reached for the locket his grandfather had given her to rub its golden surface as she so often did.

"Are you certain you want to keep Miss Markham as your companion?" He hoped his grandmother would realize that having her underfoot would only be a nuisance. While a companion might be beneath a normal lord's notice, Elliott spent much of his time at home in his grandmother's company. Miss Markham would not be easy to ignore, not as lovely as she was. It would be far easier if she left. "Now that I've returned, it seems unnecessary."

"Of course, I want to retain her. You are never here even when you're in town. Besides, I am thoroughly enjoying her company. Wait until you come to know her, then you will understand."

Why did his grandmother's words feel more like a threat than a promise?

⚯

Time passed slowly as Sophia waited for a knock on the door that would summon her to the earl's library where she would be formally dismissed.

She refused to start packing as his lordship had suggested. That seemed like it would send a message to the heavens that she was willing to go when she wasn't. Not without protest.

Tired of pacing and waiting for a knock, she stepped into the hall, feeling a trespasser in what had started to feel like her home. Did she dare seek out the countess? But what if the earl was still with her?

She had no desire to show him she hadn't followed his order and risk angering him. Heart pounding, she walked downstairs in search of a footman or Codwell, hoping not to run into the earl.

When a footman advised her that the earl was in his library, she breathed a sigh of relief. Surely that was a good sign.

She hurried up the stairs to the countess's withdrawing room and knocked on the door before opening it.

"There you are, dear," the older woman said with a smile as Sophia curtsied. "I was beginning to wonder what happened to you this afternoon."

Sophia sat beside the woman of whom she'd grown so fond. "May I speak frankly, my lady?" She couldn't bear the idea of having the threat of dismissal hanging over her head.

"Of course."

"I had the...*pleasure* of meeting the earl earlier. He advised me that my services would no longer be needed now that he has returned." Sophia's stomach tightened as she held her breath, waiting for an answer.

"Nonsense. He only has his nose out of joint as you were his uncle's idea rather than his own. He likes his privacy, so I suppose the thought of someone else living here is less than appealing, but he will become accustomed to it."

Though she wanted to hug the countess in relief, she did her best to keep her happiness to a reasonable level. The idea of searching for another position when she and the countess got on so well had been worrying to say the least. "I am very pleased to hear that. Will the earl be leaving again soon?" Sophia hoped so as she found his presence quite unnerving already.

"Not for some time, I hope." She reached out to pat Sophia's arm. "Have no worries. I am certain the two of you will grow quite fond of each other."

Sophia had to clear her throat to keep from scoffing a denial. She couldn't imagine having a normal conversation with the earl, let alone growing fond of him. He was the exact type of person her aunt had warned her about. No doubt he was like her father—not to be trusted with women or money. "I'm sure," she managed at last.

"Now then I would like you to read another chapter of that mystery before we decide which gathering we're attending this evening."

She retrieved the book from a nearby table. "I thought you had already decided we were attending the Rutland's musical."

"Since Elliott has returned, I think a ball would be a better choice." She tapped her upper lip, a sign she was pondering the options. "I believe the Charrington ball will be our best choice. Balls are always more delightful with Elliott there."

Sophia hid her sigh. The last thing she wanted to do was attend a ball and watch as the earl seduced women. If that was what a rogue did at a ball. Yet she couldn't ignore the flash of heat that filled her at the idea of those jade green eyes watching her as a charming smile tilted his lips.

Berating herself, she opened the book, but wondered what the night would bring. Her best option was to steer clear of the earl and hope he forgot his wish to dismiss her.

※

Elliott scanned the crush at the Charrington's that evening, searching for one of his contacts. He intended to pay a visit to Prime Minister Gladwell on the morrow, but if he had the opportunity to share some of the information he'd discovered on his trip now, he'd sleep easier.

"What a lovely surprise," a feminine voice purred in his ear.

Elliott turned to find Lady Hamilton at his side, a widow he'd enjoyed a dalliance with several years ago. Born in Prussia with a large family who still lived there, along with several Russian uncles, the lady was well connected. Internationally connected. She knew more than most of the intelligence community combined. Though beautiful, there was something sly in her demeanor he didn't care for.

Rather than the grimace he was feeling, he greeted her with a smile, taking her gloved hand to raise it to his lips. "You are more alluring with each year that passes, my lady."

She gave a sultry chuckle then bit her lower lip as her gaze roved over him. He wondered if she was picturing him naked. The woman had an insatiable appetite. "How was Paris?"

He raised a brow as he released her hand. "How did you know I was in Paris?" He kept his smile in place even as his senses went on high alert.

Her eyes widened ever so slightly. "I believe the countess mentioned it."

He'd be willing to wager his grandmother had said no such thing. The idea of Lady Hamilton speaking with her was laughable. It looked as if he'd be pursuing the lady with the hope of finding out all she was willing to share.

Girding himself for the task ahead, he widened his smile as he offered her his elbow. "Perhaps you'd care to dance?"

"I would love to." The heat in her gaze warned him of her interest.

As he glanced past her, he caught sight of hazel eyes watching him from the side of the ballroom.

Miss Markham.

She stood near his grandmother who visited with several friends. He could almost see the woman's internal struggle, torn between disapproval and curiosity as she studied him.

Which side would win? What would it be like to watch her eyes light with passion?

Part of him was tempted to find out.

But for the moment, he needed to keep his focus on Lady Hamilton to see if he could coax any secrets from her. After dancing and planning a rendezvous for later in the evening, he visited with a few acquaintances before making his way toward his grandmother.

"Aberland." Lord Baskwell greeted him as Elliott passed by. "Haven't seen you in an age."

Elliott shook the lord's hand. "Good to see you." Yet he realized almost immediately it wasn't.

He and Baskwell had attended university together, but from that point forward, their lives had taken different paths, with Elliott beginning his work for the Intelligence Office. Baskwell had become a true rogue, while Elliott only pretended.

Overindulging in drink and other excesses had taken their toll on Baskwell. His skin was ruddy, his nose already showing signs of the veins that marked those who drank heavily. Though the hour was early, the man's words slurred and he swayed alarmingly.

Was this who Elliott would become if he gave up his work and became a lord of leisure like Baskwell? Would he continue the role of scoundrel if no other purpose filled him?

The question of who he truly was without either of his identities worried Elliott.

Continuing through the crowd, Elliott reached his grandmother, greeting her as he always did, with a kiss on both cheeks, sending her friends into giggles. He always marveled at how their behavior wasn't so different from debutantes in many respects. Or perhaps they simply made less of an effort to hide their amusement.

"You look wonderful as always," he told her as he admired her deep violet gown. Though he knew she missed his grandfather terribly since his death five years ago, he was pleased she no longer wore the dreary colors of mourning. She was much too vibrant of a person for that.

"Why, thank you." Her smile lightened his heart and made him realize again how much he'd missed her.

Her attention shifted to her side. Elliott turned to find

Miss Markham. Her gaze tangled with his for a moment before she dipped into a graceful curtsy. "Good evening, my lord."

"Are you enjoying the ball?" he asked out of politeness.

"Very much. Thank you." She eased back, as though attempting to fade into the background.

If his grandmother refused to dismiss the woman, perhaps he could chase her away by making her uncomfortable. That shouldn't be too difficult as she'd already revealed her disapproval of him. He smiled at the thought of how quickly he could convince her to leave.

"Will you give me the pleasure of dancing with you?" he asked, all too aware of the twittering of the ladies surrounding his grandmother. He knew it was unusual for an earl to ask a paid companion to dance, but that was his purpose—shock.

His grandmother nodded in approval. "Do go dance with Elliott, my dear. Standing beside me all evening must bore you to tears."

"Not at all. I'm happy to enjoy your company and listen to the music."

"I insist," Elliott intervened. "Grandmother is in fine companionship at the moment." He offered his elbow.

A lovely shade of pink rose in Miss Markham's cheeks, her eyes glittering in the candlelight as she placed her gloved hand on his elbow. "Thank you."

He glanced over her gown as they walked, admiring the simplicity of the pale blue silk with its narrow ruffles. The rounded neckline revealed more of her alabaster skin. The dress was flat along her stomach, the fabric drawn into a small bustle at the back, emphasizing her delicate curves. The gown was modest, especially when compared to Lady Hamilton's. But sometimes it was more about what was hidden than what was revealed.

He should know as he'd spent the past few years seeking hidden information. He frowned at the odd thread of his thoughts this evening. Obviously, he was more tired than he realized.

As they reached the dance floor, the strains of a waltz began. He turned to face her, placing a hand on her waist and taking her hand in his. Was that a tremble he detected?

He searched for other signs of nerves, his gaze catching on the rapid pulse beating at the base of her neck. Why did he long to touch that delicate spot?

"You're enjoying the ball thus far?" The twinge of guilt he felt at her obvious nervousness surprised him. Wasn't that exactly the reaction he was hoping for?

"It is very nice." Her voice revealed nothing, her expression calm and demure. It was her eyes that gave her away—something glittered in their depths.

As he led them around the dance floor and she glided with him through the movements, the crowd fell away.

Her dark curls were drawn into an artful chignon that bounced lightly as they whirled along. He had the urge to release her so he might touch a strand to see if it was as soft as it looked. Her dark brow arched, as though wondering at his thoughts.

He gave his roguish smile, hoping to suggest he was thinking things he shouldn't be thinking in polite company.

But she either wasn't affected by his attempt or didn't believe he'd do so with her.

It bothered him that he couldn't tell which it was.

"Have you always lived in London?" he asked, when their movements permitted conversation.

"No."

He waited but when she offered nothing more, he continued, "In the country then?"

"Yes."

Usually he was more successful in convincing people to talk, especially ladies. He searched his mind for a question that wouldn't allow a simple yes or no answer.

"Aberland, there's no need for all this," she informed him.

"Please, call me Elliott."

"Very well." Her lips tightened for a moment before she continued, "Elliott."

His given name coming from her created an unexpected reaction, a shiver of awareness he hadn't expected. Unable to resist, he pressed her. "May I call you Sophia?" He wanted to repeat her name, enjoying the roll of it off his tongue.

"Of course." She acted surprised that he'd asked permission.

He supposed a true scoundrel would've made the assumption he could. That was one more mistake on his part. With effort, he dragged this thoughts back to her comment. "All this what?"

"Conversation. I am aware you would like me gone and you're aware I'm remaining for the time being." Her eyes held his. "I believe that puts us at an impasse."

He frowned, uncertain how to respond. Used to conversing in terms that often meant something entirely different, her honest approach caught him off guard. It was disconcerting.

"Shall we agree to disagree for the sake of your grandmother?" she asked.

"You have nothing to worry over from my viewpoint."

Her eyes narrowed as they circled in time with the music. "Why don't I believe you?"

"Are you accusing me of lying?" He added a touch of steel to his tone, not appreciating that she read him so easily when he had outwitted many people in multiple countries.

"Of course not, my lord." That hint of rose returned to her cheeks, deepening the hue of her eyes.

Once again, her demeanor masked her thoughts. Damn, but the woman could have a position with the Intelligence Office.

No matter. Her behavior didn't change his goal of encouraging her to quit. She was upsetting the careful balance of his life by intruding on his haven.

She had to go, despite the surprising attraction he felt toward her. Obviously, he needed to increase his efforts to make her uncomfortable.

As an idea took hold, he glanced at his grandmother to be certain she wasn't in need of either of them. His plan ought to have her gone by morning.

The music swelled as he eased her toward the garden door, looking forward to his new adversary's reaction far more than he should.

Chapter Three

Sophia could count on one hand the times she'd danced at a ball. Each one paled in comparison to this. The breathless feeling she was experiencing couldn't be solely blamed on the waltz, which meant it was because of the man who held her.

She did her best to hide her agitation, though feared she was failing abysmally. Elliott—rather, the earl—had thoroughly rattled her. Why was it she felt as if they were playing chess, where each move might well be her last?

He was everything her aunt had warned her about—a womanizer who frequented gaming hells and brothels, stayed out all hours of the night, and drank far too much.

But in this moment, he was handsome and charming. Already her understanding of how her mother might have felt about her father had shifted considerably.

Her thoughts came tumbling to a halt as the earl drew her through the open garden door, still moving in time to the music. The large terrace allowed them to take several more turns before he slowed their steps.

"I thought a breath of fresh air was in order."

She searched his expression, trying to determine what he was about. Being alone with any man was a mistake, let alone one with his reputation.

"So warm in there, even with the garden doors open, don't you think?" He tucked her gloved hand under his elbow and moved toward the shadows.

Her pulse quickened as she pondered the proper course of action to take. This was outside her realm of experience. Did she excuse herself and return inside?

As she opened her mouth to do just that, Elliott looked up. She couldn't help but follow his gaze, wondering what he could possibly be looking at.

"Only a few stars are visible. Nothing like the stars you see from the deck of a ship at sea."

Her imagination took hold at his words. "What is it like?"

He turned to look at her, the dim torchlight surrounding the terrace casting shadows over his features. "The stars or the ship?"

"Both. All of it." Her experiences were so limited she couldn't picture either.

"You must know of the stars, having lived in the country." His deep voice was quiet, sending a tiny shiver down her back as though he'd run a finger along her spine. Thank goodness his gaze returned to the night sky. She didn't want him to know what he did to her.

"The stars are beautiful in the country," she agreed. "So many more than in London. It's one of the things I miss about living there. But surely you can see even more at sea."

"I suppose that's true, as they are visible from horizon to horizon on a ship in fair weather. It's quiet as well. And peaceful. Only the occasional creak of the boat and a splash of ocean as some sea creature passes by." He turned to look at her again. "Somehow when it's quiet, you can better appreciate the sight. Does that make sense?"

She nodded, something inside her loosening at his words, as though her soul understood him in that moment. She held his gaze, wanting more of the feeling. Despite being surrounded by others, she had been very lonely since her mother's death.

Elliott seemed to sense her wish, for he continued, "It is much easier to believe all is well with the world when a blanket of peace descends upon you."

She nodded again, imagining the sensation. "Like the first snow. When those perfect flakes fall and all is quiet and renewed."

He smiled—the first genuine smile he'd given her—and caused her heart to spin. "Yes. Exactly like that."

"What else have you seen on your travels?"

A shadow crossed his face, telling her not all he'd seen had been pleasant. Then he caught himself and glanced at her. "The good things?"

"Yes. The good things." She already knew of bad things—death and broken dreams, heartache and sorrow. And loneliness. Those she'd either experienced firsthand or received endless lectures and warnings about. In this moment, she only wanted to hear of the good things.

He looked back at the night sky as though seeking inspiration. And his memories. "Paris is delightful. The coffee there is thick and rich, the aromatic smell adding to the taste. The *Arc de Triomphe* stands tall, but creates chaos with the traffic." He shook his head. "Luckily the shelling by the Prussians during the Siege of Paris didn't destroy it."

Sophia couldn't help but study him, surprised he mentioned the war. "That ended only a few months ago."

"In January. Did you know they transported mail by balloons for a time?"

"Truly?" She tried to picture it.

"Balloons and pigeons."

"Isn't that clever?"

"They're building a tram in Madrid. It will be pulled by mules and is supposed to open next month."

"You've travelled to so many places. Where else brings you that feeling of peace?"

He paused for a long moment as though to give her question serious consideration. "*La Almudena*, Madrid's Catholic Church next to the palace. Ardgroom Stone Circle in County Cork, Ireland, although it has an eerie quality as well. One feels restless spirits there."

All those places sounded mysterious and wonderful to her. Reading about such sights wasn't the same as seeing them.

"What of you?"

His question took her by surprise. The way he watched her suggested he truly wanted to know, that he wasn't merely being polite. "I haven't ventured anywhere except between my previous home and London."

He frowned. "Surely you've seen the ocean?"

She shook her head. Her aunt hadn't approved of such frivolous travel with no purpose. Nor had there been the funds to do so.

Elliott turned to face her, so close she could feel the warmth of his body, feel his breath on her cheek. Awareness curled through her, catching her by surprise.

His gaze held hers, and she couldn't have looked away if she'd tried. "If the opportunity presents itself, you must go. Somewhere you can stand upon the beach and watch the surf pound the shore. The power of the ocean is invigorating. You will find peace there as well."

In her mind's eye, she saw only the gentle lap of the waves of a pond against the bank. Envy tugged at her.

Though she knew she was lucky to have a roof over her head and plenty of food, she longed for so much more. That feeling frightened her. How many times had her aunt reminded her to be grateful for what she had? She had no desire to live with unfulfilled wishes like her mother. No—that hadn't been living. Merely existing.

Nor did she want to live her life dissatisfied, like her aunt. That wasn't truly living either.

Elliott reached out to run a finger along her cheek. "You would love it."

As though he'd cast a spell, she stared at him, feeling as if he could see into her thoughts, deep down to her most hidden desires.

Then he edged closer, his gaze dropping to her lips. She froze, unable to believe that what she thought he was going to do was actually correct.

But it was.

He took her lips with his, slow and gentle just as his words had been. Yet neither of those qualities matched what she felt. As though he'd struck a match, something within her burst into flame, heating her deep inside.

His lips were firm and sure, his head moving as though to coax a response from her.

With a moan, she drew nearer, wanting more of this. How was it possible to feel so much? To want so much? When his tongue ran along the crease of her lips, she startled, parting her lips in surprise. Then his tongue swept into her mouth and all thought stopped.

This...this was magic.

His arms wrapped around her. Her body tingled. Everywhere.

Emboldened by the feelings coursing through her, she returned the kiss with equal vigor. Her gloved hand reached up to touch his cheek.

Then the voice of Aunt Margaret sounded in her ear, admonishing her for her reckless behavior, telling her she was no different than her mother. *Wickedness loves company.* How often had Aunt Margaret repeated that and many other proverbs?

Sophia drew back, shocked at herself.

At him.

At the desire flooding her body.

For the briefest moment, she saw the surprise in Elliott's jade green eyes in the torchlight. He hadn't been expecting whatever this was either.

Then a shutter drew over those eyes. Once again, he was a scoundrel, a knowing smile on his face as he eased back.

"Well. That was...unexpected." His gaze swept over her as if he saw her in a new light.

How ironic, since she now viewed herself in a new light as well. She had never expected to be tempted by a scoundrel.

"We had best see how my grandmother is faring."

She nodded, fearing her voice would emerge as a squeak, or worse, a moan.

Within a few short minutes, Elliott returned her to his grandmother's side, his rakish smile in place as he walked away.

"I trust you enjoyed the dance?" The countess glanced at her.

"Yes. It was lovely." Curse him, for it truly had been lovely, as had the conversation and the kiss afterward.

The other women shifted the countess's attention, much to Sophia's relief.

"What a wonderful ball."

Sophia turned to see her cousin, Dalia Fairchild, at her side. "Isn't it?"

Dalia's eyes narrowed as she studied her. "What's happened?"

"I don't know what you mean." Sophia feigned interest in the crowd, hoping Dalia would change topics.

"I may not know you well but even I can tell something is amiss." Dalia stepped closer, the skirt of her lavender gown brushing Sophia's. "Do tell."

"Nothing to report. I danced and am slightly out of breath."

"With whom?"

Goodness, but Dalia was like a dog with a bone. A hint of news and she latched onto it for all she was worth. "The earl."

"The earl? As in, the Earl of Aberland? He has returned?"

"What other earl would dance with me?"

Dalia tapped Sophia's arm. "You underestimate your own charms."

Sophia scoffed. "You truly don't know me well."

"Sophia." Dalia's tone was full of reprimand. "I refuse to allow you to speak of yourself that way. Now, back to the matter at hand. How was the dance?"

"She says it was lovely." The countess leaned around Sophia to look at Dalia. "What do you suppose that means?"

Sophia wished the floor would open and swallow her whole. The countess's hearing was far better than she would've guessed.

"Good evening, my lady." Dalia curtsied before responding. "I have to wonder what it means as well. She tends to use that word frequently."

"I noticed that too." The countess gave one decisive nod, as though Dalia's agreement pleased her.

Sophia shook her head at the pair. "What would you have me say?"

"Additional details would be helpful. After all, you have only had a handful of dances." Dalia leaned forward, her gaze on the countess. "Wouldn't you agree?"

"Indeed."

Sophia could only sigh. It was going to be a very long evening for more than one reason.

※

Elliott followed Lady Hamilton's footman into her withdrawing room later that night. If his luck held, he'd be leaving shortly. He had no desire to engage in a dalliance with the lady, but neither could he afford to have her sharing the secrets she held with anyone else.

Her international connections could provide interesting information. Unfortunately, her price for telling him what she knew might be higher than he cared to pay.

"Aberland, how nice of you to come by." She waved

away the footman, who closed the door as he left.

Elliott greeted her with a kiss on the cheek, hoping he wouldn't have to do much more than that. The woman's sexual appetite was not exaggerated.

Her attire had him concerned. The smoky grey nightgown and matching robe with its plunging neckline revealed more than it covered. He did his best to keep his gaze elsewhere in case what he thought was fabric was actually skin.

"Pour us a drink, will you, darling?"

He moved to the sideboard that held several crystal decanters. "Sherry?"

"Something stronger, please." She fingered the teardrop diamond that dangled between her generous breasts, drawing his gaze though he quickly looked away.

He poured them both brandy, handed her one, and took the chair near the settee where she sat before the fire. "How was the remainder of your evening?"

"Dear Elliott, there is no need to play games with me. I know why you're here."

Alarm filled him though he did his best to hide it. Had his long-kept secret been discovered? He quickly considered his options, hoping he could control the damage this would cause.

She took a sip then offered him a sultry smile. "We have many mutual interests."

He smiled, delaying a response by taking a drink of his brandy until he knew to what she was referring.

"But tonight, I am only interested in one," she continued, cupping the glass in her palm. She looked up at him from under her lashes and bit her lower lip.

In his younger days, he might've been interested in what the lady suggested. He'd indulged himself more often than he should've with the excuse that it was part of the requirements of his position.

But not anymore. He'd grown tired of that life. He wanted more—if only he knew what *more* was.

She shifted from her place in the center of the settee to the side and patted the seat next to her. "Come closer, darling."

He complied, still uncertain what topic she was discussing. Until he knew, he wasn't going to assume anything. The time had come to make his own moves in this cat and mouse game they played.

Holding his glass, he sat and placed his arm over the back of the settee near her shoulders. "I'm so pleased to have a few moments alone with you. With my travels keeping me away from London, I am behind on events, including those pertaining to you."

"I'm flattered you care." She ran a bold hand along his thigh.

He lowered his arm so he could caress her shoulders then stared into her eyes. "Tell me."

Compliments worked wonders with this woman. She chatted easily, telling him of trivial matters. Relief filled him as he realized she hadn't been referring to his work with the Intelligence Office.

He held onto his patience with the hope she'd reveal something noteworthy. A few well-timed questions and feigned interest in her every word brought the conversation around to her uncle, who was deeply involved in Russian politics.

As he'd suspected, the Russians were concerned with Prussia's growing power. But that didn't mean they were prepared to side with Britain over anything. Anarchists were active in every country from what Elliott had learned over the years. Many viewed Britain and its ever-growing empire as an unwelcome force that had to be stopped, including the Russian anarchists.

Russia was a country of such vast diversity and distances it was only natural that certain individuals there sought freedom to rule their own people and believed others should have that right as well. Great Britain's policy of expansion was unwelcome.

But the chaos anarchists created had no place in Britain's well-ordered government. Any activities they planned were only intended to harm. Innocent lives would be lost and that could not be tolerated.

"You are so devoted to keep in close contact with your family despite the distance separating you." He ran a finger along her neck. "Family gatherings must be interesting with the varied countries represented."

Each time the conversation paused, her hand wandered higher on his thigh. If he could keep her distracted and talking, he might learn more and keep her hand from moving.

After an hour more, he decided he'd learned as much as he was going to. The woman was like an octopus, reaching for him so frequently he'd been hard pressed to stop her. He'd convinced her he was weary from his travels and didn't want to give her a poor performance in bed and left with no more than a few kisses.

As he closed the door of her residence behind him, he couldn't help but wipe his mouth. Lady Hamilton might be experienced, but there was no doubt the kiss he'd shared with Sophia had been far different—far better—than anything this lady offered.

When he closed his eyes in his own bed as the fingers of dawn crept over the horizon, it was Sophia, her expression full of wonder, who filled his dreams.

Chapter Four

Sophia sorted through a basket of thread as she visited with the countess. Three days had passed since that unexpected kiss with Elliott. He'd been gone most of the time, much to her relief. The notion of facing him again was enough to make her shift uncomfortably in her chair.

She had no idea what had gotten into her that allowed her to return his kiss the way she had. The memory heated her cheeks with embarrassment.

The longer he stayed away, the better, though she knew he returned home to sleep each night. Or should she say each morning? How he managed to get by on so little rest was a mystery to her. Then again, that wasn't the only mysterious quality to the man.

"I'll need some bright red thread as well. Is there any in the basket?" the countess asked as she examined the needlework she held.

"Yes, I saw it only a moment ago," Sophia said, grateful for the request. Anything to distract her from her thoughts. The less time she spent thinking about the earl, the better.

Her aunt had insisted Sophia avoid idleness at all cost. *Idle hands are the devil's workshop*. In truth, Sophia knew her mind rested easier when her hands were busy, whether it be with needlework or some other task.

Mornings like this with the countess were her favorite time, when the streets were quiet and no visitors required clever banter with which she felt inept, especially when the callers rarely said what they meant.

Most days, she remained out of the conversation during calling hours, certain the countess had no interest in her companion's thoughts on anything. But more often than not, the older woman drew Sophia into the discussion, seeking Sophia's opinion on a variety of issues.

Sometimes the conversation was merely a recap of the fashion or behavior they'd witnessed at the previous night's event. Other times, the talk delved into political issues. Much of it Sophia found fascinating, but some of it seemed petty and trivial.

"Did I mention we're having supper with Elliott this evening?"

Sophia's stomach fell as her gaze flew to the countess's. "Oh?"

"I would like the two of you to become better acquainted. Then maybe he'll stop hinting that I no longer need you."

"I'm sure supper will be delightful." Nerves simmered as she realized the precariousness of her position had not yet been resolved. She'd hoped that by avoiding the earl, he'd have forgotten all about her. Apparently, that was not the case.

"I expect you to be your usual charming self so he might see you for who you truly are."

"I look forward to it." Though she had no intention of allowing Elliott to see her true self. Her sheltered life couldn't possibly be of interest to him. No, she'd have to pretend to be different than who she was if she wanted him to like her.

And she had to find a way to cover her distaste for his roguish behavior. It was none of her business if he stayed out late every night or if his clothes reeked of cheap perfume, brandy, and cigars. At least, that was what she'd overheard the maids saying.

She was far from perfect. Who was she to judge anyone? Still, the idea of spending the evening with his watchful gaze on her made her nervous.

"Try to engage him, my dear. Be friendly."

Sophia offered a small smile, hoping not to choke. If only the countess knew how friendly she'd been with Elliott the other night, she wouldn't be so encouraging. "I will do my best."

"That's all I ask."

All too soon, it was time for callers. Sophia served tea, visited when necessary, and tried to anticipate the countess's wishes. The afternoon passed quickly and soon Sophia was in her room, dressing for supper.

She took care with her appearance, though she didn't know why. The idea of dressing to please the earl was nothing a proper companion would do. Besides, he wouldn't notice anyway. Would he?

Annoyed with herself and her doubts, she focused on the purpose of this evening—to gain Elliott's approval. The thought only brought another flurry of uncertainty. It seemed an impossible task when they were already on the wrong foot. The interlude they'd shared had been so brief it didn't count. Except for in a secret corner of her soul.

She paced her room, trying to think of safe topics of conversation. Safe but interesting. Oh, dear. This was impossible. Nothing in her life thus far had prepared her to be an engaging conversationalist to an earl.

Yet she had no choice. She needed him to like her if she wanted to keep this position. It was only for one evening. How difficult could it be?

Armed with a very short list of topics and renewed confidence, she descended the stairs to the drawing room.

The earl and the countess were already in attendance, the earl standing near his grandmother's chair. Their gazes swung to her as she entered. Her confidence flew out the window but still she curtsied and offered a greeting. Already she felt the weight of his regard.

"You look lovely this evening," the countess offered.

"Thank you." She smoothed her gloved hands down the front of her pale pink gown, grateful her cousin was not only the same size but also had good taste. "As do you, my lady."

But as she said it, her gaze shifted to Elliott.

"Why thank you," he answered with a cocky smile.

Heat rushed to her cheeks. "I meant—"

"Sophia dear, don't allow him to ruffle you." The countess waved a hand at her grandson. "Elliott! Behave yourself."

"I only responded to her compliment." He grinned and moved to the sideboard. "May I offer you a sherry?"

"No, thank you."

"Pour her one anyway, Elliott," the countess insisted. "It's good for the nerves."

He did as requested and handed the glass to Sophia. "Grandmother's orders."

Sophia smiled as she took the drink, trying to think of a clever response. Something that sounded interesting. Where was her natural wit when he was near? "My aunt didn't allow any spirits in the house. She was certain it would lead to trouble. Then again, she believed anything pleasant would lead to trouble." Too late, she realized how inane her comment was.

To her relief, Elliott chuckled. "Living with your aunt must have been a challenge. How long did you stay with her?"

"My father passed when I was six years, so my mother and I went to live with her sister. Then when my mother died two years later, it was just my aunt and me." Though her memories of her father were vague, she had recollections of a handsome man laughing, lifting her high, bringing light to her life whenever he came home.

Unfortunately, he had rarely come home.

Her mother's happiness had revolved around her father's infrequent visits, her sorrow apparent long before her father died. Aunt Margaret took 'I told you so' to a new level with her comments and lectures and dire warnings about men and the evils they represented.

"I'm sorry to hear of your loss. My parents died in a carriage accident when I was ten years of age." He glanced at his grandmother. "We have been depending on each other for many years, haven't we?"

The countess smiled. "I'm grateful you allow me to live here with you instead of sending me to the country."

"Why on earth would I do that? I don't want to rattle around in this house by myself."

"Soon you will need to focus on seeing to the business of an heir. You won't want an old woman in the way during that."

As Sophia wondered if she should make some excuse to step out of the room as the conversation was growing personal, Elliott knelt beside his grandmother.

"You will always be welcome here." He took her hand and squeezed it. "Always."

Sophia's heart twisted. His kindness toward his grandmother conflicted with everything else she believed about him. If only he always acted as a rogue, it would be easier to reconcile her feelings toward him.

Now what was she supposed to think?

The conversation continued to lighter topics, including the evening engagements over the next few days and which ones the countess wanted to attend.

Sophia was just beginning to wonder when supper would be announced when the countess rose.

"I fear I'm going to have to leave you two to proceed without me. I'm not feeling myself and think I'll retire early."

Sophia's heart sank. She didn't like the idea of the countess feeling poorly, but neither did she care for dining alone with the earl. "Why don't I accompany you? I'll have the meal sent up to your room and we'll eat together."

"No need. Codwell will see to it. You two enjoy dinner."

"Allow me to escort you upstairs," Elliott said as he offered his elbow.

"Don't fuss." The countess's order was softened with a smile. "I am fine. Just tired."

Sophia watched as she stepped out of the room, wishing that by pure force of will she could convince the older woman to return. But no. The countess disappeared, calling for Codwell. Sophia dearly wanted to follow her.

She felt the weight of Elliott's gaze and waited, not looking at him, certain he would make an excuse to leave. But when the footman stepped in to announce dinner was ready, Elliott turned to her.

"Shall we, Sophia?"

When he said her name, she had no choice but to shift her gaze to him. He gave her that smile—the one she didn't like as it wasn't real—and offered his arm to escort her to the dining room.

This was going to be the longest meal of her life.

※

Elliott wanted to curse his grandmother. Her color was good and the light still sparkled in her eyes as she'd left. He was certain she feigned feeling unwell so he and Sophia might have a chance to come to know each other better.

He disliked disagreeing with his grandmother. But he didn't care for another set of watchful eyes upon him either. Deflecting Sophia's attention away from him and his activities should be something he did without a second thought. He was a spy, after all. His life was built on doing that very thing each and every day. But it was exhausting, especially of late. He needed the brief time he spent at home to be relaxing and free of pretending.

A glance at the woman on his arm as they made their way to the dining room did not encourage relaxation.

At the top of his mind was that kiss. As many women as he'd kissed over the years, the act was rarely memorable. But that kiss with Sophia had been stunning.

The past few days had been busy, filled with meetings with fellow officers of British Intelligence, the prime minister, and his contacts in the seedier part of London. He'd met with his Uncle Daniel to chastise him for suggesting his grandmother have a companion, but it had been difficult to press his point when his uncle had commented on how happy his grandmother was now that she had Sophia.

Despite all his activity, his most frequent thoughts had been of kissing Sophia. His mind drifted toward her no matter what he was doing. It was distracting.

If he could chase her away, surely these thoughts would go as well.

She looked less than pleased at being left alone with him. He was tempted to make an excuse and leave, but he had no doubt his grandmother would be displeased if he did so. That could not be easily dismissed. No, the coward's way out wouldn't be worth the aftermath.

Perhaps if he behaved improperly, he could convince Sophia to quit, leaving his grandmother none the wiser.

A footman stood near the entrance of the dining room, prepared to serve them. The table was set for two, making him believe his grandmother had never intended to dine with them.

With his plan in mind, he realized the seating arrangement would never do as the place settings were at either end of the long, polished table.

"Will you please move the settings together?" he asked the footman before flashing a smile at Sophia. "That will allow us to better converse." He patted her hand as he escorted her to her chair.

There it was—that subtle tightening of her lips that

spoke volumes of her poor opinion of him. This was going to be easier than he thought. She'd be packing her bag this very night. He'd console his grandmother by taking her shopping or some other outing she'd enjoy.

He gestured for the footman to pull out the chair for Sophia, watching as disapproval flashed across her face because he hadn't seen her to her chair. Hiding a smile, he took his place at the end of the table beside her.

The first course was served. Elliot watched as Sophia ate, her manners impeccable.

"Lovely day, wasn't it?" she asked. "We walked through the garden between visitors this afternoon."

He frowned. He'd grown used to her not speaking unless spoken to. What was she about?

"Did you have a chance to enjoy it as well?" She held his gaze, her expression one of polite interest.

"Briefly." He bit his tongue before he mentioned anything about the many meetings he'd had. That would only make her curious as to why, and he couldn't share that.

"Mrs. Fairchild and two of her daughters came by. They are relations of mine and acquaintances of your grandmother. Do you know them?"

He skimmed through his mental files until he recalled Mr. Fairchild. "I believe we've met. How are they related to you?"

The conversation continued with Sophia surprising him with the topics she raised. She spoke intelligently of recent political events, popular books, and the ramifications of so many country dwellers moving to the city. He wasn't certain when he'd had a more stimulating evening.

"What did you think of *The Seven Curses of London*?" he asked.

"The bookshop hasn't yet received it."

"I look forward to hearing your thoughts on the curses."

Before he knew it, they were ready for dessert, and he

had yet to make her uncomfortable in any way. What was wrong with him? Apparently, he was distracted even when he was *with* her.

He drained his glass of wine and motioned for the footman to pour him another. That ought to upset her. Not that he intended to over imbibe. He merely wanted her to think he had.

As the footman cleared away their dishes, Sophia turned toward him. He had no doubt she intended to make her excuses and retire for the evening. He wasn't about to let her go yet.

"Join me in the library," he requested, giving her a grin that should surely set her lips twitching.

Dismay flickered across her features.

Perfect.

He escorted her toward the library, where the fire burned cheerfully. After seeing her to the settee, he poured himself a drink, not bothering to offer her one. Surely that would be another black mark against him.

Dangling the crystal glass from his fingers, he moved to the fire. "You and grandmother are attending another ball tomorrow evening?"

"I believe she wanted to attend Lord and Lady Campbell's ball."

"I hope to come as well. Perhaps we'll have the chance to dance again." He sat beside her and took her hand.

"That's kind of you, but I know how busy you are."

"Never too busy for my grandmother's companion." He set aside his glass and ran his fingers slowly along her arm until he reached the soft skin of her inner elbow. He circled his finger in a pattern, noting the slight tremor of her arm. He raised his gaze to meet hers. "I look forward to dancing with you again."

Rather than the concern he expected in her expression, she appeared perplexed. That was not the reaction for which he was hoping. She studied him as though searching for a solution to a puzzle, her hazel eyes curious. He had the unsettled feeling she saw past his façade.

Frowning, he tried again. "Perhaps we can share another private moment afterward."

She glanced about. "We're rather private now, aren't we?"

Her reminder only proved how much he was off his game. Why make promises for what might happen when he could do what he wanted now?

"Yes, we are." He leaned close, hoping to intimidate her into backing away. But once again, she seemed more curious than fearful.

Why did she never act as he expected? It was maddening. Now, more than ever, he wanted to fluster her. To make her feel as out of sorts as he did.

This sensation was precisely the reason he wanted her gone. He needed to focus on the information he'd gathered abroad and follow the leads he'd uncovered in recent days. He didn't have time to worry over what she might be thinking or seeing.

His gaze dropped to her mouth, but he was surprised that true desire now prompted his movements.

Before Sophia had come into his life, it had been a long time since he'd kissed a woman solely because he wanted to.

"Sophia." He caressed her arm as his lips neared hers. His eyes closed as he drew in her presence with his senses.

Suddenly, she was gone.

He opened his eyes to see she had risen to stand before the fireplace, facing the flames rather than him. While pleased he'd at last flustered her, he regretted her escape even more.

"The balls are nice, but I also enjoy the musical performances." Her quiet words took a moment to sink in as he was so focused on that *almost* kiss.

He retrieved his glass and rose, taking advantage of her turned back to dump the drink into the potted plant near the sideboard. Then he took care to rattle the crystal stopper in the decanter as he poured another drink.

His ploy worked, for when he turned back to her, she faced him, her gaze on his glass.

He deliberately took a sip before approaching her once more.

"What of you?" she asked, obviously still trying to be a good conversationalist. No doubt his grandmother had told her to.

"I appreciate some performances more than others." He raised a brow as he moved closer, hoping to suggest he wasn't referring to music or any other polite society event.

"Such as?" Her head tilted slightly as though curious as to his answer.

He reached her side and ran a finger over her shoulder and down her arm. "Such as the one playing right now." He kept his voice low as he continued. "I wonder if you'll let me closer." He edged nearer. "If you'll allow me to kiss you once more."

Sophia's eyes grew wide. "Oh?" If he wasn't mistaken, she sounded rather breathless.

That made two of them.

He tilted his head, ready to take her lips with his, wondering how far he might take this kiss. When her hand moved against his chest, his body tightened with anticipation, only to realize that hand was firmly pressed against him with an entirely different purpose than he'd wanted—to halt him.

A glance at her face confirmed it. She was having none of this. She took a step back. Then another.

"I've appreciated our time together this evening." She looked deliberately at the drink he still held. "But I would like to check on your grandmother before the hour grows too late."

She dipped into a curtsy and was gone before he could think of a reason to protest.

He scowled, realizing he didn't care for the sensation of failure. Especially not at something he was supposed to be good at—playing the role of scoundrel.

The enigmatic Miss Sophia Markham was proving to be more of a challenge than he'd anticipated. Damn if he didn't look forward to their next encounter.

Chapter Five

Sophia woke the next morning, a knot of dread lodged in her stomach. She gave into her mood and tugged the covers over her head, not wanting to face the day.

No doubt the earl intended to convince the countess to dismiss her based on her behavior last night. She'd tried to be friendly and interesting during supper, but the earl had deliberately attempted to provoke her.

It confused her when he acted like such a scoundrel. How could that man be the same one who'd held his grandmother's hand and declared his affection for her with no worry over how his behavior would be perceived? The man who had spoken to her of the stars and his travels had been different as well. Which man was true?

His reputation was known far and wide and bandied about in polite society as a well-known fact. Who was she to wonder if it was a falsehood?

Besides, what reason could he possibly have to encourage the rumors of his exploits? No advantage of doing so came to mind. If anything, she thought he'd prefer to act in a manner that would make his grandmother proud.

Of course, Sophia knew the countess loved him dearly. They shared a special bond. It would take more than his outlandish behavior to dim their affection.

With a sigh, she pushed back the covers. Lying here wondering if she needed to pack her bags wouldn't change the outcome. Better to proceed with the day. Until she was dismissed, she had duties to attend to.

Most of all, she wanted to find out how the countess fared. Sophia had looked in on her the previous night but the light was out in her room, suggesting she already slept.

As Sophia dressed, she considered Elliott's behavior throughout the past week. Something was off, but she couldn't place her finger on it. Finally, it struck her. He didn't act like a man whose sole purpose in life was to have a good time. Rather he moved through his days with determination, his thoughts seeming to be on weightier matters than whom he might ravish next or where to find the liveliest entertainment.

If he were truly a rogue, wouldn't he have followed her to her room last evening or tried to accost her in the middle of the night while she slept? She'd heard stories of maids and governesses who awoke in the dark of night to find the master of the house on top of them.

She couldn't imagine Elliott doing any such thing. His careless acts—those he did without forethought—always reflected his kindness and respect for others. It was his deliberate movements, such as the way he'd advanced on her last night, that suggested improper behavior.

With a shake of her head, she reminded herself that her opinion didn't matter. She was a companion in this household. Not a guest. Not a relative. She was paid to be here, and she'd fare better if she could remember that.

It had been her choice to become a companion. After living with the extremes of her mother's broken-hearted existence and her aunt's bitterness, she was certain this was the best option for her. She couldn't risk being hurt and living as unhappily as they had.

She glanced in the mirror to make certain she was presentable, tucked a loose curl of hair into her chignon, pinched her cheeks to help hide the fact she'd had a restless night, and left her room, hurrying down the stairs.

Only to run directly into Elliott.

He reached out to catch her, holding her bare arms.

"I'm terribly sorry, my lord."

"I'm not." His easy smile drew her notice, causing a slow heat to fill her.

His green eyes were clear and he smelled wonderful—nothing like a man well into his cups the previous evening would smell.

He continued to hold her lightly, and she couldn't find it within her to step away. Not when he looked at her as if pleased to see her.

That couldn't be the case. She'd refused his advances last night when she knew he wanted her gone. Why wasn't he angry or at least annoyed?

As though aware of the questions circling her thoughts, the warmth in his gaze cooled as a layer of reserve shuttered his expression. He reached up to slowly run a finger along her cheek then down her neck. The corner of his mouth tilted up, but she recognized it to be a false smile.

Why did he act this way?

The answer came easily but still unwelcome—*to convince her to leave*.

Disappointment filled her. Why did he want her gone so badly? Surely the little he'd become acquainted with her hadn't made him dislike her that much.

From what she could perceive in this moment, with the warmth of his finger trailing along her skin leaving tingles in its wake, she had two choices.

She could either comply and leave, as he so obviously wanted her to do. Or she could choose not to let his forward behavior bother her. That would be easier said than done when his touch, his glances, his smiles—the genuine ones—set her heart racing.

One fact at the heart of the matter guided her decision. She wanted this position. She adored the countess and enjoyed spending time with her. The older woman was so different from both her mother and her aunt. Sophia felt valued here, and the countess seemed to like her.

For the first time in a long while, Sophia was happy. She had to find a way to stay in Elliott's good graces so she could keep her position.

"Are you going to see your grandmother?" With a bright smile, she stepped away from his finger, trying to ignore how bereft she felt without his touch. "That's where I was going as well. May I accompany you?"

Without waiting for an answer, she moved down the hall, glancing over her shoulder to see him standing right where she'd left him. "Aren't you coming?" she asked.

"Yes, of course." A frown now marred his brow.

She turned to hide her smile, pleased she was keeping him off balance as much as he was her. Perhaps this day held more hope than she'd thought.

Later that morning, Elliott considered each word carefully as he penned a message at the desk in his library to one of his associates.

Writing down information was always a dangerous endeavor. One never knew who might intercept the message, yet it needed to contain enough details to be helpful. Meeting with each and every person with whom he needed to communicate wasn't practical. He'd already been overextended in his activities since his return home.

That was surely the reason Sophia had gotten under his skin. He'd been thinking of her, and when she practically fell into his arms in the hall, he'd been delighted. But playing the role of rogue with her had become a chore as it required significant effort.

Her reaction this morning had been surprising. She'd ignored his advances as though not bothered by them at all.

He tapped the top of his desk, pondering the moment again, trying to focus on her odd reaction rather than the softness of her skin.

No matter how he felt toward her, she remained a threat to his identity. The simplest way to remove that threat was to remove her. Unfortunately, that was proving to be far more difficult than he'd expected.

Suddenly aware of a presence at the door, he looked up to find Codwell waiting patiently, holding a silver tray with a message. At Elliott's nod, the butler walked to his desk and held out the tray. "This arrived for you, my lord."

The symbol on the front identified it as having been sent by Prime Minister Gladstone. "Thank you." He took the missive reluctantly. He didn't know what it contained, but no doubt it held either unwelcome news or additional work.

Codwell had been with him long enough that he knew a few details of Elliott's work. He never asked questions but occasionally offered bits of gossip and rumors that crossed his path from other households.

If the *ton* realized what their servants knew and how often they shared it with others, they'd more closely guard their secrets. Didn't they wonder what the footmen discussed as they waited for their lords and ladies at balls or what was whispered between maids who crossed each other's paths on their daily jaunt to the market?

It was impossible to hide everything, but Elliott did his best. He trusted Codwell and knew he could count on his discretion. Elliott had no doubt the servant knew who'd sent the message, regardless of who'd delivered it.

"If I may mention a trivial matter, my lord?"

Elliott looked up at Codwell's request. "Of course."

"It might be best if you avoid pouring your drinks into

the palm. The plant doesn't care for it." He nodded toward the pot Elliott had emptied his drink into the previous night.

Codwell was correct. The palm appeared wilted, as though ill from too much alcohol. Elliott had felt the same on more mornings than he cared to count. Now, he did his best to dump the liquor rather than drink it so he didn't feel as the plant obviously did.

"I have taken the liberty of placing a decorative pitcher on the side table and another beside the fireplace with the hopes that they will provide you with an alternative."

Elliott nodded in amusement. "Well done, Codwell. We wouldn't want to kill any plants, would we?"

"I believe that one was a gift from your grandmother. She would be disappointed with us if that occurred."

Elliott chuckled. Codwell was right. Luckily, she didn't come into the library often. He hoped she didn't visit until the palm recovered.

A soft knock at the open door caught his attention.

Sophia cleared her throat. "I'm sorry to interrupt, but your grandmother is hoping for a word with you in her withdrawing room when you have a moment."

Elliott stared at Sophia, wondering what she'd overheard. This proved that he needed her gone. Keeping secrets was no easy task, especially not with a curious, intelligent woman living in his house.

But he knew beyond a doubt he was going to miss her when she was gone.

※

Dalia looped her arm through Sophia's as they walked along Bond Street. "I'm so pleased you suggested this outing."

"When the countess requested I pick up a few things for her, I thought it would provide the perfect opportunity to spend time with you." She smiled at her cousin. "Plus, I know you know the best places to find everything on my list."

Dalia laughed. "Ah. The true reason is revealed. I am only here for your use."

"That's not true and you know it."

"It's quite all right. I have another purpose as well."

"Do tell." Spending time with Dalia and her sisters always brightened Sophia's mood. She enjoyed their company. They reminded her how to relax and release her seriousness.

After only a few minutes in Dalia's company, her worry eased. The tension between her and Elliott was starting to wear on her. Their constant battle of wits over the past few days was both invigorating and exhausting.

"I wanted to hear how you're getting along with the earl."

"What do you mean?" Sophia cursed the heat filling her cheeks.

"Come now, Sophia. You danced with him. You had a private moment on the terrace with him. You live with him. And he is a scoundrel. All of that adds up to *something*. Is he behaving himself or do you have to beat him away with a stick?"

The mischievous glint in her cousin's eyes had Sophia laughing. "It's a good thing I know you are jesting."

"I'm serious. You're an attractive single lady. He's one of the *ton's* most eligible bachelors, well known for his roguish ways. I have no doubt you are a temptation he has difficulty resisting."

"Please. I'm his grandmother's companion. What interest could he possibly have in me?" Other than to convince her to quit. In truth, she was hurt by the idea that he wanted her to leave—hurt enough that she decided against sharing it with Dalia.

Her plan to ignore his advances had been successful the past two days, but it didn't change her disappointment at his wish for her to leave.

"Fine then. Keep your secrets." Dalia lifted her chin, a teasing light in her eyes. "Obviously, we're not as close as I thought."

Sophia gave her a gentle push with their linked arms as they walked. "You are being ridiculous."

If anyone had secrets it was Elliott. Though she hadn't meant to eavesdrop, she'd heard Codwell's comment about the palm in the library. The very one he'd been standing near the other night just before he'd refilled his glass. Had he truly poured his drink in it? Why would he want her to think he was over imbibing?

As she considered the matter, she became even more convinced there was more to the earl than met the eye. She vowed to watch him closer from now on to see what he was up to.

If she dared.

After all, watching him more risked increasing the attraction she already felt for him. Was she strong enough to resist it?

Dalia chuckled in response. "Very well then. If you're not going to tell me anything exciting, let us proceed with our shopping. What is first on your list?"

With Dalia's assistance, she purchased lace, buttons, and a different shade of red thread for the countess's needlework project.

"Do you mind if we stop by the bookshop?" she asked her cousin. "A book we ordered came in."

The bell of the shop tinkled as they entered. Sophia breathed in the slightly musty smell of books, loving the promise it represented. There hadn't been bookshops in their small village in the country. It required great effort on her part to keep from wandering up and down the aisles to see what treasures awaited.

Concern for the countess kept her focused on her purpose. Sophia didn't want to be gone long. The older woman seemed especially tired earlier and intended to rest while Sophia was gone. Sophia was anxious to make certain she was well.

The shopkeeper retrieved the book they'd ordered and slid it across the counter for her inspection. "Here it is."

Sophia ran her gloved hand over the embossed, leather-bound cover in appreciation. She was looking forward to reading this and discussing it with the countess. "Yes, this is the one."

"Truly? You're going to read *The Seven Curses of London*?" Dalia asked as she picked up the book. At Sophia's nod, she shook her head. "My sister, Lettie, talks about this book frequently."

"Really? She liked it then?"

"She's gone so far as to try to solve one of the problems the author notes. That's how she and her husband met. At the foot of Blackfriars Bridge, where she was attempting to convince some of the young girls who worked in the factories to allow her to assist them."

"How marvelous." Sophia tried to imagine having the courage to do such a thing. "That is so brave. Do you think she would speak with me about it?"

Dalia narrowed her eyes. "You will lose at least an hour of your life by raising the subject. She's impossible to stop once she starts."

"Perhaps the countess would like to invite her to tea. I'm certain she'd enjoy hearing of your sister's activities as well."

"Do me the favor of not inviting me when that occurs. I have heard the stories too many times already."

Sophia envied Dalia her large family. Though she knew Dalia sometimes felt she blended in with her sisters, loneliness would never be a problem with so many siblings.

After the shopkeeper wrapped the book and they departed, Sophia asked, "Do you ever have the desire to see if you can make a difference?"

Dalia was quiet for a long moment as they strolled along, her expression serious. "I confess the idea of another Season of the same balls and parties and musicals doesn't hold the appeal it did last year. It all seems rather frivolous after you learn of the problems others face."

"I can see why you might feel that way."

Pausing on the walkway, Dalia added, "Please know that I mean no offense, but your life hasn't been an easy one, has it? It sounds as if you and your mother and aunt got along on very little."

"I didn't mind going without so much as when Aunt Margaret made us feel guilty for taking pleasure in anything. Laughter was a rarity in our world after we went to live with her when Father died." She realized now that her father was a combination of traits, not exclusively good or bad. Weren't all people, including Elliott?

"I can't imagine that." Dalia shook her head. "I hope you are finding chances to enjoy your new life."

"I count my blessings every day, and you are one of them."

"I feel the same of you." Dalia's smile warmed her heart.

Sophia truly loved her new life and the people in it, but she knew she needed to tread carefully. The stakes were high, especially with Elliott.

Chapter Six

Elliott shrugged on his suit coat in the library, his thoughts on the evening ahead. He had to make an appearance at three different events followed by a meeting with a brothel madam, but first he had an appointment with two associates from the Intelligence Office.

His work over the past few days brought forth hints of an alarming plot by anarchists to send a bold message to the Empire. With luck and a little prodding of certain parties, he hoped to gain enough information about the anarchists' plans to identify both their target and the timing of their attack.

The message he'd received earlier today from Gladstone advised that Her Majesty wanted an update on the situation. In order to prepare for that, he needed more details, hence the meetings.

There had been a time in his past when he would've reveled in the challenge of the night. But this evening, he only felt weary and worried. Weary of making the rounds, doing all he could to prevent a problem when another simmered on the horizon. Worried that despite all his efforts, innocent people would die as he hadn't been clever enough to recognize the signs of what was to come.

He would much prefer an evening at home. His

grandmother had been under the weather the past two days and that concerned him as well. Though she insisted it was nothing, the normal sparkle in her eyes had dimmed. He didn't care for that.

"My lord?" Sophia's quiet voice from the doorway caught his attention. Her hands were clasped before her, her expression solemn.

"How kind of you to see me off." He gave a cocky grin as he strode toward her. He'd done his best the past few days to advance on her the rare times he saw her, renewing his efforts to encourage her to quit. Not that it seemed to be working.

She ignored his comment. "May I please have a moment of your time to speak with you about the countess?"

He dropped the façade without a second thought. "What is it? Has her condition worsened?"

"Perhaps not worsened, but I wonder if the doctor should see her."

The worry in Sophia's expression increased his own. "I spent a little time with her earlier. I suggested that as well, but she insists she only needs rest."

"I was told the same." She managed a smile but it didn't reach her eyes.

"She seems to think the housekeeper's homemade remedies are more helpful than anything the doctor would prescribe."

Her gaze held his for a long moment. "I wanted to be certain you were aware of the situation before you left for the evening. I'm sure you'll be quite late."

The disapproval in her tone was undeniable. Rather than pleasing him, since that had been his goal of late, it only added to his guilt. Perhaps he should find a way to stay in this evening.

"My lord?" Codwell stood just behind Sophia. "The carriage is waiting."

He felt pressed between two impossible

responsibilities. His meeting with the other intelligence officers shouldn't take long and was of vital importance. Perhaps one of them could assist him with his other commitments.

As though sensing his tension, Sophia stepped closer to reach out a hand to touch his arm, only to pull back. "I'll do my best to keep watch over her. And I will notify Codwell if anything of significance occurs."

For once, he was pleased she was here. How selfish of him to want her gone when he was rarely home. Why shouldn't his grandmother have someone to keep her company? Certainly, she had friends who visited and she was always surrounded at social events, but her time at home should be just as enjoyable.

He hated to think of her as lonely. It bothered him more than he could say.

At the moment, none of that mattered. He'd have to wait until later to decide if he truly approved of Sophia staying. For now, he was grateful for her presence.

"I'm pleased you're here to watch over her." He could at least offer Sophia that. "I will return as soon as I can."

Her lips pursed and her gaze dropped as she backed away and sank into a curtsy, as though placing both physical and emotional distance between them. He realized without a doubt he didn't care for it.

She departed before he could say anything more.

"Will you please check on the ladies this evening, Codwell? If Grandmother doesn't show signs of recovery by the morrow, we'll send for the doctor."

Codwell raised a brow. "I hope you'll be the one to advise her of that. She won't be pleased."

"Have no fear. I will take the blame." In short order, he was riding away in the carriage, but his thoughts remained at home.

"Shall I read more, my lady?" Sophia knew the countess's interest in the new mystery they were reading had waned.

She seemed unable to rest, as though she couldn't find a comfortable position. Her face was flushed, but she told Sophia she didn't have a fever. In all honesty, the countess made a poor patient. She refused to admit anything was wrong.

"I believe I have heard enough for now." She sighed and turned her head to look toward the window. A distant expression came over her face, making Sophia wonder what she was thinking.

"Can I get anything for you?"

"Do not fuss so, Sophia. I am merely under the weather, not dying."

Sophia couldn't help but smile. That sounded more like her usual self. "I am well aware of that. But I don't care for it when you're not feeling well. You are normally so vibrant."

The countess chuckled. "My husband often used that word."

"You must miss him terribly." The countess spoke of the old earl fondly. They'd obviously enjoyed their life together. It was difficult for Sophia to appreciate such a thing from what little she remembered of her mother and father.

"Five years. I still miss him every day." She turned to look at Sophia. "Elliott is very much like him."

"No wonder the two of you are so close."

"I'm sure that has something to do with it. He's a good man, my Elliott. Just like his grandfather." She chuckled again. "He plays the part of a scoundrel like my husband did."

Sophia didn't understand why the countess found that so amusing. Why wasn't she angry that her husband had been a rogue and that Elliott followed the same path?

Something in her expression must've revealed her

confusion, as the countess added, "Sometimes there is more to people than meets the eye."

She met the countess's gaze, wondering what she was trying to say. Unfortunately, she said nothing more, only giving Sophia an enigmatic smile. "I think I will rest for a time."

"Shall I return to check on you? We could have supper here if you would like."

"That would be nice." Her eyes drifted closed, the hint of a smile still on her face.

Sophia left quietly, hoping sleep would prove restorative for the countess. She'd grown very fond of the woman and much preferred her previous vitality than the shadow she'd become the past few days.

Restless, Sophia remained in her room for a time then ventured down to advise Codwell of the arrangements for the evening meal. Next, she went to the library to find something to read to distract her from worrying.

As she perused the shelves, she was amazed once again at the variety as well as the organization of the books. Had Elliott collected them? Some were quite old while others were new. Books on farming techniques and land management. Classic Greek and Roman texts. Some so old she didn't want to risk pulling them from the shelves for fear they might disintegrate.

The selection of fiction near Elliott's desk by the windows offered new and old books, mysteries, romance, and adventure. The choices were overwhelming. Despite that, she couldn't set aside her unease at invading Elliott's personal space. He spent what little time he was at home in his library.

Well aware it would take an intriguing story to hold her attention this night, she took her time. She pulled down several books and set them on the desk to take a closer look. A note fell from between the pages of one, fluttering to the floor under the desk. Dismayed that she might have lost someone's bookmark, she bent to retrieve it.

Something else caught her eye as she reached for the fallen message. Another missive was stuck in a narrow space, where the wood joined to form the inside corner of the desk.

Curious she tugged the note free and unfolded it before she thought twice. The writing had a masculine look to it. The note was brief, signed only by a single initial.

H.M. requests an update.

G.

What on earth did that mean? She shook her head, annoyed at herself. She shouldn't be reading the notes, yet she couldn't help but open the one that had fallen from the book.

The second missive was written in a feminine slant, the loops wider than the first note's writing. The idea of it being from one of his many conquests made her hesitate, but her gaze swept over the words regardless.

A.

Additional details have arisen.

Meet me at my home this evening. Midnight.

L.H.

She reread the swooping letters. That didn't sound like a simple rendezvous with a lover. Details? What sort of details? Heart racing as she cursed her inquisitive mind, she examined the other joints of the desk but did not open any drawers. That was a line she wouldn't cross.

Nerves fluttering, she glanced at the door, expecting Elliott to stride into the room and berate her for spying on him. Yet no one entered. That didn't slow her pounding pulse.

When the desk didn't reveal anything further, she turned back to the books, doing a quick search of the volumes by tipping them toward her to see if any additional notes were hidden. She found nothing more on the shelves before her, so she moved along, randomly searching as she went.

Overcome by guilt, she soon gave up her quest. She

wasn't meant to spy—her nerves couldn't take it. She returned to the desk, reading the notes one more time. What did they mean? Why had he saved them? Or was it simply that one had been used as a bookmark and the other had fallen?

Added to these were the countess's words about how there was more to Elliott than one might think. Along with her own questions and observations, what conclusion could she draw?

None that she could see.

Though frustrated with the lack of answers, she refused to search further. Elliott's activities were none of her business. She returned the note to the book and tucked the other one into the crack in which it had been wedged. The messages only added to the mystery of the earl and who he truly was.

His reputation as a rogue surely had merit based on facts. Why else would he travel so often, if not to enjoy gambling and women in distant cities? Yet she knew he enjoyed spending time with his grandmother. She couldn't deny the times he'd spoken with her and the genuine connection she'd felt with him.

Elliott was a puzzle. Each time she thought she understood him he did something unexpected. The curious notes only added to her confusion.

She made her selection and returned the rest of the books to the shelves. Reading no longer sounded appealing but pondering Elliott's conduct would serve no purpose either.

After spending a restless hour in her room, she went to look in on the countess. Light shone under her door, so Sophia opened it slowly, not wanted to wake her with a knock if she was sleeping.

To her surprise, the bed was empty. When she opened the door farther, her surprise turned to horror. The countess lay crumpled on the floor, unmoving.

Elliott braced himself as he entered the brothel on Church Street late that evening. It didn't matter that this was a more refined establishment, catering only to lords and diplomats of a certain status. It was still a brothel.

In his younger days, he might've enjoyed the amenities offered but the more he visited these the less tempted he was. This evening was no exception.

He had lingered in the lower rooms of brothels often enough to realize few of the women were pleased to be there. He knew Prime Minister Gladstone made a habit of walking the streets at night to convince prostitutes to find a new way of life.

Elliott wondered if something more could be done to help. While these women were perhaps more fortunate than their counterparts who worked on the streets, they were still prostitutes. He would mention it to Gladstone when next they met.

As he waited for the madam, concerns over his grandmother tugged at him, along with the memory of the expression on Sophia's face as she'd bid him good evening. He often felt torn when his duties took him away, but tonight was far worse.

His previous meetings had raised additional concerns, hence his visit to the brothel. Several sources pointed here. The madam had been recruited to assist in collecting intelligence three years ago and had proven helpful, especially with the diplomats who visited her establishment. Men often bragged of their activities after a drink or two in mixed company, despite the delicacy of said activities.

The décor was exactly as one might imagine, red velvet drapes, gold and crystal chandeliers, and touches of dark mahogany. Ostentatious was all Elliott could think as he waited in the drawing room.

The woman who escorted him into the room had

poured him a drink, but he refrained from drinking. Remembering Codwell's words, he avoided pouring it into the plant and dumped a good share into a vase of flowers instead.

With luck, the madam would be forthcoming with information, and he could share it with his contacts and return home within the hour. He shook his head. Since when had he become an optimist? It would take at least two hours before he was done with all this.

Guilt flooded him. The matters he'd uncovered could not be dismissed lightly. Innocent lives were involved, yet all he could think of was how long it would take before he could go home.

Perhaps he was no longer the best person for this position. Spying was a dirty business. Few of his peers were willing to admit it was needed let alone participate. The government was loath to fund intelligence work. At some point, more formal action needed to be taken, starting with the Queen.

For now, Her Majesty preferred to think of those in the Intelligence Office as loyal men who happened to come across the information they collected rather than actively gathering it. 'Spying' was a term to be avoided. Thankfully Gladstone understood the situation and found a way to pay those working in the office as well as reimburse them for the information they had to buy, else Elliott's coffers would've been seriously reduced by now.

Before he could consider the matter of his future further, the door opened.

"What a delight, my lord." Josephine Blakely sank into a graceful curtsy, a suggestive smile curving her lips.

An attractive woman in her fifties, she'd inherited the brothel from her aunt. Ambitious, well connected, and intelligent, she'd taken the modest operation and moved up her clientele's standards.

Her efforts had paid off in spades from what little Elliott knew. She now received additional funds for catering to foreign diplomats who frequented her establishment, not to mention the money she received from the British government for any intelligence her girls gathered.

"I appreciate you seeing me on such short notice."

"To what do we owe the honor of this visit? You so rarely grace us with your presence."

"I'm hoping you can assist us with a situation." He raised a brow, wondering if he needed to clarify further.

"Of course." She glanced at his empty glass. "Perhaps we could share a drink upstairs in my personal drawing room so we might *visit*. In *private*." The emphasis she placed on the words made Elliott smile.

Her methods of "visiting" were known far and wide. Her skills in the boudoir were unmatched, if one listened to the gossip. "I'm afraid I must keep my visit brief, but I would appreciate a few moments of your time."

She bit her bottom lip while her gaze swept over him. She appeared disappointed with his answer. No amount of sultry looks from her would change it, but he took care not to offend her. She could change sides as easily as a tree swayed in the wind.

"Come along then." She reached for his hand, surprising him. "We must keep up appearances."

He nodded, allowing her to guide him through the foyer. A few other men he recognized mingled with their chosen ladies for the night. One nodded as they passed, while others pretended not to see him.

No wonder his reputation as a scoundrel continued to spread. Moments like this added to it. With a resigned sigh, he escorted Josephine up the stairs to her suite. She unlocked the knob with a key tied to her wrist.

Releasing a melodic laugh, she pulled him through the door and locked it behind her. Her expression sobered as she released him. Apparently, that had been for show. "Now, shall we have that drink?"

"Allow me." He made his way to the polished table

that held crystal decanters of various shapes, eyeing the liquids to determine which she might prefer. Sherry seemed too mild for a woman such as she. "Brandy?"

She smiled, as though pleased he'd guessed. "Perfect."

He poured them both a short one, hating to waste the woman's liquor since he had no intention of drinking it.

"Now then." She settled onto a settee before the fire and patted the tufted cushion beside her. "What may I help you with, my lord?"

Though he knew her to be a trustworthy source, that didn't mean he could come straight out and ask. People rarely said what they meant and often times, they interpreted things differently than someone else who heard the same information.

"I've heard disturbing rumors and am interested in learning if you have heard them as well."

She raised a brow as she took another sip, watching him over the rim of her glass. "You already know I'm happy to help our government."

Unless another entity offered her more.

But he kept the thought to himself. She was in business and he respected that, as long as it didn't interfere with his mission. This cat and mouse game was a challenge—getting the other party to talk without revealing too much of what he knew was never easy or straightforward.

"Your assistance is appreciated. I thank you on behalf of Her Majesty." It never hurt to name drop and remind her of whom they served.

The woman's eyes widened at the mention of the Queen. "My pleasure."

Elliott gave her a charming smile. He'd learned from the start that flattery and flirting were a requirement in these situations. "Rumors have surfaced that certain Russian factions intend to send a brash message to the Queen."

"The Russians are always so...passionate. I believe they often mistake the British reserve for indifference." She set her glass on a side table and trailed her fingers along his arm. "But that couldn't be further from the truth, could it?"

"Has the Russian diplomat who frequents your establishment mentioned anything?" He did his best to ignore the hand moving slowly along his chest.

"He was here a few days ago. He mentioned that many activists would like to see Britain slow their empire building and concentrate on the problems within their own borders rather than continuously expanding."

It took far longer than he'd hoped but Josephine at last revealed that she expected the Russian to visit again on the morrow. Now that she understood where to lead the conversation, she might have more luck in gathering details.

When it became clear she knew nothing else, at least nothing she was willing to share, he eased into his goodbye.

"I do wish you would stay for a time now that we have concluded business." She looked at him from under her lashes, sliding her hand along his shoulders. "Though I see only a few clients myself these days, I would make an exception for you."

"I'm afraid I must respectfully decline."

Her lower lip protruded in a pout. "Are you certain? We could spend an enjoyable few hours together."

No doubt her skills in the boudoir surpassed the majority of his previous companions, but he wasn't tempted. Thoughts of Sophia and worry over his grandmother held all his attention.

"It would certainly be a memorable evening but duty calls."

"Duty? Or a woman?" She studied him as she asked.

Sophia's image immediately filled his mind.

"Ah. I see the answer. A woman has caught your eye." As he shook his head, she placed her hand along his cheek to still him. "No need to hide your interest. Pretending it doesn't exist doesn't make it go away."

Was that what he'd been doing? Masking his attraction to Sophia with his attempts to chase her away? He'd excused his behavior by telling himself he was trying to convince her to leave. Somewhere along the way, that had no longer become true.

"Is this a surprise to you?" She smiled, as though delighted she'd helped him.

"Perhaps." That was as much as he was willing to admit.

Josephine had obviously become adept at reading others. In truth, that was how she made her living—anticipating men's needs and wants before they admitted them.

And Josephine was very good at her business.

"May I offer you some advice, my lord?" At his reluctant nod, she added, "Do not wait. Life is short and so often unexpected events occur." A shadow passed over her features, leaving him to wonder what had happened in her past. "Grab any chance of happiness with both hands and do not let go. Not even for Her Majesty."

To his surprise, her words echoed in his mind as he rode home in a hansom cab. Was that what was at stake with Sophia? Happiness? Something in his chest twisted at the thought.

The word had become foreign in his life. He couldn't deny the feeling that washed through him each time he came upon Sophia, as if his heart leapt at the sight of her. He'd thought it simple anticipation of their battle of wills.

How ironic that a conversation with a brothel madam had caused such a deep revelation in his life.

Yet the question remained—-what should he do about it?

Chapter Seven

Sophia remained at the countess's bedside, waiting for the doctor, her stomach knotted with worry. Hours had passed—the clock in the hall had struck midnight—but the elderly woman had yet to regain consciousness, and the doctor had not yet arrived.

Sophia had no idea what to do. She feared the countess's illness had not only worsened, but that she'd injured herself when she fell. Her odd position on the floor suggested she might've twisted her hip or leg, and a red bump marked her hairline. Sophia surmised she'd hit her head on the small bench at the foot of her bed.

Codwell and two of the footmen had gently returned her to the bed, but still she hadn't woken. Sophia berated herself for leaving the countess's side. She should've insisted on remaining in the room while she rested.

How she wished Elliott would return. Codwell had sent for the doctor and was kind enough to offer reassuring comments to Sophia, but she wanted Elliott.

The idea of losing the countess when she'd grown to care so much for her was devastating. The older woman filled a void in Sophia's life she hadn't realized existed until these past few weeks. The countess was like the grandmother she'd never known. They shared a love of books, of knowledge, of life.

The countess made Sophia feel like an intelligent, clever individual. No lectures, no heartbreak, only a joy for life. There was no drama as there had been at home with her mother, father and aunt. Not that she didn't love and miss her family. This was just...different.

She shifted as the door opened, disappointed to see it was only Codwell once again.

Elliott, where are you?

Her silent question went unanswered. Of all nights that he stayed out late... What was she thinking? He stayed out late nearly every night.

"The doctor should arrive any moment. No doubt she'll be most displeased with us for sending for him." Codwell stood near the end of the bed, his watchful gaze on the countess.

"We shall tell her she left us no choice." Sophia was aware her words lacked conviction, but until she knew the countess would make a full recovery, worry held her tight in its grasp. "I should have remained with her, in case she needed something."

"Nonsense, Miss Markham. The countess has a strong will and does not take kindly to anyone opposing her."

Sophia appreciated his attempt to make her feel better, even if it failed.

A footman opened the door. "Doctor Brown has arrived."

Sophia rose from her chair by the bed as a grey-haired man with spectacles and carrying a black leather satchel entered.

He glanced briefly at her before looking at Codwell. "It must be serious if she requested me to visit."

"She is unaware of the request as of yet," Codwell advised. "Miss Markham, her new companion, found the countess unconscious on the floor a short time ago."

The doctor nodded at her then stepped closer to the

bed, setting his case on Sophia's vacant chair. "Fell? That's not like her."

"She's been feeling poorly for the past two days," Sophia added. "A bit of a cough and quite weary."

As the doctor examined her, Sophia and Codwell eased back to allow some privacy.

Before the doctor finished, Elliott strode into the room. "What happened?" His accusing glare landed squarely on Sophia.

Guilt flooded her as she stepped forward to explain. "She fell—"

Before she could offer anything further, he brushed past her to his grandmother.

"My lord." The doctor bowed to Elliott then continued his examination, easing aside the countess's hair for a closer look at the bump. "I understand she's been under the weather of late."

"She insisted it wasn't anything a few days' rest wouldn't cure."

"Stubborn," Doctor Brown muttered. "There's a bit of a congestion in her lungs. We'll need to keep a close eye on that."

Sophia debated stepping out of the room, wondering if now that Elliott was here she should leave. But she couldn't bear to until she knew the countess was going to be all right.

"I'll leave something for her cough in case she needs it." He looked at Sophia. "Can you describe her position when you found her?"

Sophia closed her eyes for a moment as the shock of that moment filled her before advising how the countess had been lying.

The doctor gently lifted each of her feet, bed covers and all, checking to make certain everything moved properly. "I don't believe she's broken anything, but we won't know for certain until she wakes."

"Why hasn't she?" Sophia asked, unable to keep from

wringing her hands.

"Difficult to say." The doctor shook his head. "Might be from striking her head."

Elliott winced at his words.

"Or her illness may be worse. Perhaps a combination of the two. She has a fever, but it isn't high enough to be of grave concern. Can someone sit with her? I would like to return when she wakes and do a more thorough examination, though it might not be until the morrow. She might sleep through the rest of the night."

Elliott escorted the doctor from the room, Codwell behind them.

Sophia settled into her chair beside the countess, determined to remain there until she woke. While she felt better now that the doctor had seen her, her worry wouldn't ease until the countess opened her eyes.

Within a few minutes, Elliott returned. Sophia braced herself for a reprimand, but he had eyes only for his grandmother.

His hair was disheveled, a sign he'd run his hand through it. "How long?"

"I'm sorry?"

"How long was she on the floor?"

"I don't know." Sophia's stomach clenched. That very question had circled her thoughts more times than she could count. "As long as an hour. We were visiting and her restlessness seemed to have eased at last when she spoke of your grandfather. Then she asked me to leave her so she might rest. I don't know why she would've risen from the bed after I left."

With a sigh, he walked over to the dressing table. "She must've wanted this." He lifted a gold locket by its chain from the table. "My grandfather gave this to her on their first anniversary. When she misses him, she holds it. She says it brings him closer."

"I've seen her with it before, but I didn't realize its significance or I would've gotten it for her before I left."

She shook her head. "I should've insisted on staying."

Elliott placed the locket on the bedside table before turning to Sophia. "You and I know there is no point in arguing with her. She is a woman who knows her own mind."

Sophia looked up at him in surprise. He didn't blame her?

"What?" He cocked a brow at her.

"I thought you were angry that I hadn't prevented her fall."

He drew near and took her hand to help her rise. "Prevented? Are we speaking of my grandmother?"

"She does have strong opinions." Her aunt would've berated her to no end for an event like this, regardless of whether it was truly her fault or not. The idea that Elliott didn't was both a relief and a puzzle.

"If the two of you are going to speak ill of me, the least you could do is go into the other room." The roughness of the countess's tone spoke of the congestion the doctor mentioned.

Sophia thought nothing sounded sweeter.

"Grandmother." Elliott released Sophia and hurried to the bed to take her hand. "You gave us a scare."

"Me as well." She touched her head, wincing.

He retrieved the locket from the table. "Were you wanting this?"

She smiled wanly as she reached out a trembling hand to take it. "Yes. I must've lost my balance."

"Are you in pain?" he asked.

"My hip aches nearly as much as my head, but not compared to my pride." She coughed, the nasty rattle causing Sophia to meet Elliott's worried gaze.

"The doctor left something for your cough." Sophia pointed toward the brown bottle on the nightstand.

"I'd much prefer the remedy the housekeeper makes. It doesn't make my mind as foggy."

"I'll ask her to make more," Sophia offered. "Then I

will sit with you for the remainder of the night."

"No, no, my dear. Have Sally sit with me tonight so you can stay with me tomorrow."

Sophia glanced at Elliott. The countess agreeing to have someone stay with her all night proved how poorly she felt. "As you wish, my lady."

"Sally doesn't read as well as you do." The countess gave her a weak smile. "I am most anxious to continue reading *The Seven Curses of London* to see what else Mister Greenwood discusses. I don't believe Sally will appreciate his observations."

"I look forward to it." Sophia gave the countess's hand a gentle squeeze. "I'm so pleased you've woken. I'll return shortly with your drink."

With a quick nod at Elliott, she closed the door then leaned against it for a moment, saying a prayer of gratitude.

※

Elliott closed his grandmother's bedroom door, pleased she was resting comfortably after drinking the warm brandy with honey and lemon the housekeeper had prepared. How he hated seeing her looking so fragile, a shadow of her normal self.

If only he'd returned home sooner, circumstances might be different. Guilt was a constant companion of late. Aware he was too restless to sleep, he went down the stairs to his library, only to encounter Sophia in the hall.

"I just spoke with the housekeeper to see if she had any other remedies that might aid the countess."

He gestured toward the library door. "Why don't you have a nightcap with me and tell me about it. You look as though you could use something to calm your nerves." As she opened her mouth to protest, he added, "I insist."

"But your grandmother—"

"Is asleep with Sally at her side." He held open the door, pleased when Sophia acquiesced and preceded him into the library.

The fire still burned, as if the footman had anticipated Elliott would use this room before retiring.

He poured her a small glass of sherry and a brandy for himself, thinking how different this was from his previous drink with a woman. Josephine and Sophia couldn't be more opposite. Being with Sophia was like drawing a deep breath of fresh air, and he appreciated it more than he could say.

Sophia sighed as she took the sherry. "I'm relieved to hear that. The housekeeper had one or two other possible remedies she promised to make on the morrow. She's determined to assist in the countess's recovery but is unwilling to share the ingredients. All she would tell me is that the recipes were handed down from her grandmother."

"I hope she's sharing them with someone. Whatever will we do once that generation and their wisdom passes away?" The idea of that happening to his grandmother caused a catch in his throat.

It had been terribly difficult when his parents were killed and again when his grandfather died. But losing his grandmother might be the worst of all.

Sophia moved toward the fire, the glass cupped in her hands. "My mother knew little of such things. My aunt had no knowledge either, though her cook made us a terrible drink when we had an upset stomach." She shuddered. "Thick, nasty green-colored stuff that smelled as if she'd mixed peppermint leaves in pond scum."

Elliott drew nearer, feeling his tension ease. "Did it work?"

"In all honesty, I was never brave enough to drink it. I tossed it when she wasn't looking." Her gaze swung to the withered palm.

"It's recovering already." The words slipped out before he could think better of it.

"Why?" Her focus shifted to the glass in his hand.

"Why what?" he asked to give himself time to think of an answer.

"Why pour a drink if you don't want one?"

"I want this one." As though to prove it, he took a small sip.

She raised a brow, clearly dissatisfied with his response.

"There are times when drinking is expected of me, but I'd prefer to have my thoughts clear." He cursed himself. Why did he feel compelled to tell her the truth?

"I see."

That was the problem. She saw and understood far more than he wanted her to. As he'd known from the start, having her here was dangerous.

From her curls that were always trying to escape her chignon to her hazel eyes that reminded him of the sea glass he'd found on a distant shore, to her intelligence combined with an education that surpassed many men in his acquaintance, Sophia was a force.

A very attractive force.

She enticed him more than any woman he'd met throughout his travels. He simply couldn't help himself.

Now that he'd given up trying to gain a reaction from her, he was thinking of other things. Things like the curve of her upper lip, the pert tip of her nose, the length of her dark lashes, and the smoothness of her skin.

"Do you?" he whispered as he stepped closer, hoping she wouldn't retreat.

Did she truly *see* what she did to him?

Her watchful gaze met his. The scent of her, a mixture of lilacs and the sea, filled his senses. Her freshness was like a heady wine, something to be savored and enjoyed.

The fire cast shadows and light alternately over her face. He had no idea what she was thinking.

Her gaze dropped as if she realized he spoke of something different. Then just as quickly, she straightened, her eyes catching his as her chin lifted. "I do. I've learned that things are not always as they seem. Appearances can be deceiving. Don't you agree?"

Did he dare say yes or would that reveal too much? He couldn't risk her guessing his secrets. Could he?

His focus dropped to her lips and all questions fell away. All thought fell away. Except for one—the taste of her. He lifted a finger to touch her lower lip, but her quiet gasp only increased his need to kiss her.

He couldn't stop himself any more than he could stop the moon from rising or the stars from coming out at night. He took her mouth with his. Sweet yet spicy. Gentle yet strong. She was a mix of contradictions, and he was grateful she'd entered their lives. His grandmother wasn't the only one who'd come to care for her.

He eased closer still to draw her into his arms, loving the feel of her against him. The touch of her fingers against the hair at the back of his neck sent desire pulsing through him. He eased his hands to her narrow waist, wishing he could feel *her* rather than the layers of clothes.

Just as he deepened the kiss, Sophia drew back.

"Elliott?" Her whisper paused his movements.

"Yes?" He did his best to calm his passion. No doubt she intended to call a halt to this. He braced himself.

"You feel divine."

Chuckling, he placed a hand along her cheek. "I was thinking the same of you."

She mirrored his movements, and he tipped his head toward her hand on his cheek, her touch deepening his need for her. With a groan, he wrapped his arms around her and kissed her again. He parted his lips, hoping she'd do the same. When she did, he swept his tongue against hers.

She stilled for a moment as though surprised, then joined in the kiss.

What was it about this woman that inflamed his senses so? He had no doubt she was innocent, but the way she responded to him made him want to carry her to the settee and have his way with her.

Instead he eased back to look into her eyes, tucking an errant strand of hair behind her ear, determined to enjoy this interlude. "Will you sit with me for a time?"

Those wide hazel eyes blinked at him. "Of course."

With her hand in his, he guided her to the settee and sat beside her, taking her in his arms once more. "Your skin is so soft," he murmured as he kissed her cheek then down her neck.

"Oh?" The breathlessness of her response, along with the way she tilted her head to allow him better access, sent his need for her spiraling deeper.

He kissed her, his tongue sweeping more forcefully against hers, intent on showing her how much he wanted her. Again, she matched his movements.

More. He wanted so much more. He reined in his desire but gave into the urge to run his hand along her jaw and down her neck. Continuing his exploration, he eased over her collarbone, her pulse there quickening as he caressed her. The smoothness of her skin drew him, and he moved closer to the modest neckline of her gown.

"Oh. My."

"So perfect." He watched her as he lowered his fingers to caress the top of her full breast, back and forth, until he reached his goal. The tip of her breast was taut, growing tauter still as he touched her.

Her head fell back on a sigh, eyes closed, cheeks pink with desire.

The way she responded to him had his body pulsing with need. But no. Sophia was a woman to be wooed and won, not to be used for a quick toss. Knowing he gave her pleasure was enough for the moment.

He eased down the neckline of her gown and lowered his hand to lift her breast free, desperate to see her. The rosy tip beckoned, and he dipped his head to place gentle kisses along her supple skin until he reached her nipple. His tongue circled the tip repeatedly before at last suckling her.

Her moan was his reward.

Shifting to the other side, he gave her other breast the same attention. Her passionate response tightened his body painfully until he throbbed with desire.

"Elliott." The way she uttered his name was part demand and part plea.

It didn't matter which as he was happy to continue. He sought the hem of her gown, wanting closer contact. He ran his hand along the length of her leg, pleased to find every inch of her as soft as her breasts.

He kissed her again as he continued his journey to her thigh, shifting aside her undergarments to touch her bare flesh.

Her tight embrace felt like heaven as her tongue swirled against his. When her clever fingers unbuttoned his suit coat and vest, he realized how much he wanted her touch. "Yes, my sweet," he urged as he eased back.

"I want to see you. To touch you."

He wanted her so much he feared his need might frighten her. He shoved it back once again, telling himself he wanted a few more minutes before stopping this madness.

In short order, she'd unbuttoned his shirt to caress his chest. Nothing had ever felt so good. He wanted her to experience that as well. He lightly skimmed her warm, delicate skin. The scent of her arousal made him ache.

As he grew closer to the center of her body, she drew back.

"Elliott." Her eyes had darkened with passion but her brow creased with worry. "This is...wonderful. A true gift." She seemed surprised at her own response. "But I can't do this."

He wanted to tell her she was wrong. That she was doing it very well. But no matter how much he wanted her, he respected her and her wishes, even if he was tempted to try to change her mind.

She adjusted her gown as he watched, but he wished

she were removing it instead.

To his surprise, she reached up to place her hands on his face, holding him still. Then she kissed him, her tongue reigniting his desire threefold. After several delightful minutes, she pulled back, resting her face against his.

The sweet gesture had something in his chest loosening, twisting, hurting.

Then she was gone, the door closing gently behind her. Though he told himself it was for the best, deep inside, he wanted more. Until he determined exactly what that was, it would be wise to keep his distance from the tempting lady.

Why did he doubt that was possible?

Chapter Eight

Sophia rose early, having tossed and turned most of the night. She wrapped herself in a robe and pulled her chair to the window that overlooked the dim street.

Delivery men's carts plodded past. Dustmen with their fan-tailed hats, baggy flannel jackets, and red breeches drove by in a high-sided cart. "Dust-ho!" they called out to notify the servants they were near if the household rubbish needed to be emptied.

But none of that distracted her from her worry.

Elliott had awakened a passion within her she hadn't known existed. All her life, she'd never understood why her mother had married her father. Why she'd stayed with him after he'd been unfaithful. Why she'd loved him.

Now she knew.

It had been nearly impossible to leave Elliott's arms. Her heart twisted in protest as she'd done so. When she was with him, he made her believe happily-ever-after was possible. She'd wanted to see what making love with him would feel like as much as she wanted to breathe.

But the memory of her aunt's warnings over the years had stopped her from giving into her passion.

Sophia was well aware of the dangers of being with a

man out of wedlock. She'd be ruined if caught or if she conceived a child. Finding another position would be impossible.

After her mother's death, Aunt Margaret revealed that Sophia's mother had been intimate with her father prior to their marriage. She said it was only by the grace of God that her father had married her, otherwise she might've been forced into a life on the streets. If a woman had neither money nor a family who supported her, her only means of survival might be prostitution.

Sophia shuddered at the thought of being labeled as a "fallen woman" like those described in *The Seven Curses of London*. While her life hadn't been easy compared to some, it would be far worse if she were ruined.

Yet part of her believed with all her heart that Elliott was a man of honor. He might have a reputation as a scoundrel, but she knew him. At least, she hoped she did.

She closed her eyes, leaning her head against the cold windowpane as she remembered an argument her mother and Aunt Margaret had when they first went to live with her. Despite her father's philandering and leaving them penniless, her mother still loved him. Aunt Margaret told her she was a fool. Sophia's mother disagreed, insisting her husband had good intentions and never meant to leave them in such dire circumstances.

Aunt Margaret replied that words held little value. Actions were what mattered. Sophia agreed with her aunt. Pretty words and promises were empty unless one followed through and made good on them.

No matter how much she wanted to believe Elliott was honorable, he hadn't offered anything to reassure her, not even pretty words.

Regardless of the temptation, she couldn't risk giving into him, not in her precarious position. Her future was at stake, whereas he risked nothing by being with her.

A small corner of her mind worried that Elliott would dismiss her since she'd denied him. But her more logical side insisted he wouldn't do such a thing.

Though reason told her she'd done the right thing by walking away, the ache in her chest said otherwise.

She couldn't bring herself to be grateful for Aunt Margaret's dire warnings ringing in her ears, not with that ache.

As best she could, she pushed her worries to the back of her mind and dressed, suddenly anxious to look in on the countess.

It was far too early for her to be awake, but the urge to make certain she rested comfortably had Sophia hurrying to her room. Perhaps she could send the maid to bed and sit with her until she woke.

She opened the door quietly and stared in surprise, her heart melting. Elliott was sprawled asleep in the chair, the maid nowhere in sight. His dark hair tumbled across his forehead, his expression peaceful. He still wore the clothes he'd had on last evening. She had no doubt he'd spent the rest of the night at his grandmother's side.

Elliott might have the reputation of a rogue, but his actions spoke otherwise.

She pressed a hand to her chest, rubbing, but to no avail. The ache only hurt worse. What on earth was she to do about her growing feelings for him?

※

The next few days were a struggle for Elliott. He only wanted to remain home, both to keep watch over his grandmother, and to be close to Sophia.

But once again, duty called. His counterpart had come across the same information Elliott discovered. Confirming rumors was an important part of the process of gathering intelligence. When a threat was verified, it elevated in status, which justified putting more resources in place to uncover additional details.

Unfortunately for Elliott, that meant more of his time.

While relieved to know his grandmother was recovering, he hadn't managed a moment alone with Sophia.

Considering how little he'd been home, their lack of time together wasn't a surprise, but he was starting to wonder if she was deliberately avoiding him. It wasn't difficult to interpret the doubt and caution in her eyes the few times he'd seen her. Part of him wanted to pull her into the closest empty room when he next saw her and kiss her senseless to remove that look.

But the other part of him understood her confusion and doubt. He felt the same. Sophia roused feelings in him that he'd never experienced, and he had no idea what to do with them.

With everything else happening, he told himself he'd resolve things with her after the looming threat was removed, and he had time to think, to decide what he wanted.

Even to his ears, that sounded hollow. He was normally a man of action, indecisiveness not part of his nature.

As a viscount's daughter, Sophia was not only a lady by birth but also in the way she acted. If he wanted to move forward with her, he needed to consider the options carefully. With so many pressing issues vying for his attention, postponing any decisions regarding her seemed the best option.

Yet as he walked into his grandmother's bedroom and his gaze caught on Sophia, all logic flew out the door as affection took hold in his chest and squeezed. Tight.

She sat before the window, rare afternoon sunlight streaming in, lighting her dark curls with a golden glow, her focus on the thread in her lap. His world shifted, his worry over the recent threats easing. It was almost as if when he was in her presence, the world realigned. All was well as long as she was near.

The thought both excited and terrified him. And he had no idea what to do about it.

"Elliott." His grandmother's greeting from her bed drew his focus.

"I have come to see how my favorite patient is doing," he said as he kissed her cheeks.

"I would prefer a more affectionate term of endearment as I do not intend to be a patient any longer than I must. I am growing stronger by the day."

He eased back to study her. The bruise on her forehead had faded to purple. "I like the pink in your cheeks, but I don't care for the roughness of your voice."

"Sophia insists I sound as if I swallowed a frog."

Sophia's gaze met his as she rose and curtsied. The deepening pink in her cheeks caused his pulse to speed.

"I believe she is correct." They shared a smile, which only made his heart pound faster. He wasn't certain what to make of his reaction to her today.

"Do you believe she's improving?" he asked.

"Indeed, I do." Sophia shifted her gaze to his grandmother. "She insists she'll return to normal activities on the morrow."

Elliott frowned. "It seems far too early for that."

"Nonsense," his grandmother argued. "I can't continue to lie abed. I will drive Sophia to tears with boredom. Going out and about stirs the senses, you know. Quite good for one's health."

"Do you promise to return home the moment you feel tired?" He knew there was no point in arguing with her. She knew her own mind. His only hope was to encourage her to act in moderation.

"Of course. Sophia and I have already discussed this at length."

Once again, he was grateful for Sophia's presence, not to mention her level-headedness. Since he had to be gone so much right now, he didn't know what he'd do without her to watch over his grandmother.

"You've certainly been busy of late." His grandmother's tone held a note of admonishment.

Guilt resurged, though it was never far from the surface. "I expect my calendar will ease in a week or two." He wished he could tell her more. Tell them both more.

It would be helpful to discuss the details of what he'd learned to gain another perspective. A woman's viewpoint might be especially insightful. They observed different things than men.

But he had no desire to put either of them at risk. Learning of his activities might do just that. Those wishing to cause harm grew more clever by the day. He knew of two lords who'd discovered Russian anarchists working as footmen in their own home.

"So many events to attend. Busy time of the year." He gave a careless smile, aware of Sophia's watchful gaze.

A sinking feeling came over him. How could he consider having a relationship with her when he continually told her lies?

How much had his grandfather told his grandmother? Where was the line between keeping one's family safe and sharing honest communication?

"Did you hear the Royal Albert Hall is open?" his grandmother asked.

"The concert hall?" Elliott nodded. "I understand the Queen made a rare public appearance at the opening ceremony."

"My cousin's family, the Fairchilds, attended a concert last week. Dalia told us it was superb," Sophia said.

"Are you planning to attend a concert soon?" Elliott asked.

"Yes, though we haven't determined which one." His grandmother pushed herself higher against her pillows. "Sophia is acquiring a schedule so we might decide."

"Let me know which one you select. Perhaps I will invite myself along."

"We would like nothing more. Isn't that right, Sophia?"

Her companion merely nodded, not acting pleased in the least.

"I am also considering throwing a party." His grandmother tapped the bed cover with a finger as she gazed out the window. "Nothing too large, of course. Something intimate."

Sophia looked up from her needlework to watch his grandmother. Apparently, this was the first she'd heard of the plan. She glanced questioningly at Elliott.

"Not until you have fully recovered, I hope," he said.

"Of course not. In a few weeks."

"I wouldn't want you to overtax yourself with the planning and arrangements."

"I have Sophia to assist me. It has been far too long since we've held a sizeable gathering here."

He could only think of one or two since his grandfather's death, other than intimate dinners with relatives.

"Sophia should meet some young people her age."

Sophia's head popped up in alarm. "There's no need to have a party for my benefit, my lady. I'm quite content."

"Nonsense. You cannot remain a companion forever."

"Actually—"

His grandmother waved her hand in dismissal. "Despite what your well-meaning aunt told you, it's a terrible notion. There is more to life than spending time with an old woman."

"But—"

"I would like to rest for a spell, so I will ask you both to leave me for a time." She held up her finger. "I promise not to rise without calling for the maid. I won't risk falling again."

In short order, Elliott found himself standing in the hall with Sophia, perplexed by his grandmother's behavior. He studied Sophia. "What was all that about?"

"I have no idea." She stared at the closed door as though as puzzled as he.

Elliott hesitated but couldn't help himself. "May I ask what your aunt told you?"

For a long moment, he thought she wasn't going to answer. "She suggested obtaining a position and earning a wage would be the best course of action for me."

He took her elbow to steer her toward the stairs, not ready for her to disappear now that they were finally alone. "Not finding a husband?"

"She never married and frequently pointed out the disadvantages of my mother's decision to do so." She looked decidedly uncomfortable with the conversation.

Despite that, Elliott couldn't help himself. "Why?"

"My father left us in less than ideal circumstances when he died. According to my aunt, he was a rogue who spent money beyond his means on women and horses, even during their marriage."

"I am sorry to hear that. Didn't you say you were only six years when he died?"

"Yes. I don't remember him well." She shook her head as though to clear her thoughts. Or was it to deny what she did remember?

"What of your mother? What advice did she give you?"

Sophia met his gaze at last. "To never marry a scoundrel."

Before he could think of a response, she turned and hurried up the stairs toward her room, leaving him alone with his thoughts.

※

Sophia had suggested, cajoled, and argued, all to no avail. The countess would not be dissuaded from her plan to host a party. She had gone so far as to request a modiste to call upon them so they could order new gowns. The woman was to arrive that very afternoon with samples to show them.

Sophia had no choice but to enlist Elliott's aid. He didn't seem to be in favor of the party either. Unfortunately, he hadn't been vocal enough about his displeasure. If only to keep the countess from overextending herself, the party was a poor idea.

The thought of helping to host such a gathering made Sophia ill with nerves. She didn't know how to do it or how to act or...well, *anything*. Attending a function as a companion would be far different than as a—

Sophia stopped short in the middle of the hall. What would she be?

A few of the countess's comments made her feel as if she was holding the party in large part for Sophia's benefit.

No matter how many times Sophia had told her she didn't wish to find a nice young man with whom to raise a family, the countess countered with a reason why she should.

The older woman insisted Sophia's aunt had the wrong notions about life, most especially about men and marriage. "No doubt somewhere along the way, a man broke her heart."

Perhaps that was true, but it didn't change Sophia's mind. She wanted to secure her own future and not be dependent on anyone to put a roof over her head and food on the table. Granted, wages as a companion paid little, but she saved nearly everything she made. Already she had a modest amount set aside.

Elliott could change the countess's mind if he tried. While he'd said a few words of discouragement, for the most part, he'd ignored the plans.

Sophia wanted to bring the situation to his attention, along with her worry that it was all too much for his grandmother. She was becoming more and more active, but hosting a party was different from merely attending a ball for a few hours. The worrying and fussing over all the details it required would risk a setback.

Having heard him return earlier, she knocked on his library door, surprised a footman wasn't standing there. Muffled voices could be heard, but nothing she could understand. She knocked again, harder this time.

"Come." While still difficult to hear, she had no doubt of the word. She opened the door only to stop short at the sight of a shirtless Elliott before his desk, Codwell standing at his side.

Elliott's brow raised in surprise at her entrance. At least, she thought it did. She couldn't take her eyes off his body. Broad shoulders. Golden skin. Dark hair swirling over his sculpted chest. While she'd caught a glimpse of it when she unbuttoned his clothes, she hadn't seen *this*.

All thought stopped as she processed the sight before her.

Then she saw the blood.

A deep slice along his ribs oozed with it.

With a gasp, she hurried forward, not thinking of the inappropriateness of her presence, only worrying about Elliott. "What happened?"

"I thought you were the footman." Elliott reached for his shirt.

Sophia ignored him and looked at Codwell. "What happened?"

"His lordship was on the wrong end of a knife fight with no knife."

The limited answer was not nearly enough of an explanation. "Where?"

"Yes, *where* is the footman with the bandages?" Elliott asked, deliberately turning her question as he shifted in the chair, obviously in pain, holding his shirt awkwardly before him.

"I will see what is taking him so long." Codwell hurried out of the room. It was the fastest Sophia had ever seen the butler move.

"No, I—" Elliott shook his head at the closed door.

"How on earth did you end up in a knife fight?" Sophia took his shirt and set it aside then used his handkerchief to dab the blood so she could better see the injury.

"Luck, I suppose."

"You have a terrible habit of never giving a straight

answer."

"Do I?"

She glared at him from where she knelt at his side. "Yes, you do."

He only closed his eyes with a grimace. No doubt his injury hurt terribly.

"Scissors?" she asked. Apparently Codwell and the footman hadn't located any bandages as they had yet to return. "I assume this shirt is already ruined, and you won't mind if I cut it for bandages."

"Top left drawer."

She retrieved them and cut his shirt into strips. Then she took the decanter of brandy from the sideboard.

"Thirsty?" She ignored the dry note in Elliott's tone.

She created strips of bandages from the shirt, splashed some of the liquor on one of the folded strips, and pressed it against his side. Though it must've hurt terribly, his only reaction was a quiver of his flat stomach. She did her best to focus on the injury and not his bare chest. She poured a healthy dose of brandy in a glass and handed it to him.

He drank deeply before setting the glass on his desk. "Can't imagine where Codwell went." His gaze met hers. "Bandaged many knife wounds?"

"No, but I often assisted our cook in aiding villagers and farmers with injuries." She gestured for him to hold the bandage against his side then tied several strips together.

"Humph."

She examined the wound one more time then reached around him to bind the makeshift pad around his middle. "I don't think you'll need to be stitched, but no doubt Codwell is sending for the doctor."

Though she berated herself for noticing, especially when he was wounded, her gaze lingered on his muscled chest and broad shoulders. The heat of his skin beneath her hands surprised her as she reached around him several times, smoothing the strips into place.

"You are a conundrum, Sophia."

She glanced up in surprise. "Because I can bind a wound? I hardly think so."

"I don't know what to do about you." He reached out to touch her cheek.

Longing flooded her, heat rising through her entire body. "I don't know what to do about you either." She bit her lip, realizing she shouldn't have said such a thing.

"May I kiss you?" He moved his finger to lift her chin.

His eyes held hers. She couldn't deny him anything in that moment. Instead, she lifted to meet his lips, anxious for the taste of him and the glorious way he made her feel. She didn't pretend to understand what this was.

Passion? Affection? *Love?*

Her heart squeezed at the last word, as though answering her own question. No, she couldn't be falling for a scoundrel. She'd promised herself never to repeat her mother's mistake. Not after watching her grieve for her father, leaving her a shell of her former self.

Sophia wanted more than that. But she also wanted Elliott. The two seemed miles apart.

Was it so wrong to grab these few moments of pleasure? Surely she was strong enough not to lose herself, wasn't she?

When Elliott deepened the kiss, her worries fell away and sensation took over. Nothing mattered except this moment.

He eased back to kiss her cheek. "Sophia."

A knock on the door saved her from responding. She rose and eased back as Codwell and the footman entered.

Sophia walked quickly toward the door, only half listening as the butler suggested calling for the doctor while Elliott insisted he was fine.

Heart pounding, she realized she'd been wrong. Indulging in those moments of pleasure with Elliott was a mistake. For each time, he took a piece of her heart. Soon she wouldn't have any left.

CHAPTER NINE

"Is it true?" Dalia asked in lieu of greeting Sophia at the Stanford's party two nights later.

"What?"

"That the earl was injured in a knife fight at a brothel?" Her bright eyes were lit with curiosity.

Sophia's heart fell. "A brothel?" Why would he kiss her when he'd just been to a brothel? But wait. He'd arrived home in the middle of the day. Wasn't a brothel a place men visited in the evening?

Dalia held her arm, her gaze riveted on Sophia. "You seem more surprised by the brothel information than the knife wound. Does that mean you knew he was injured?"

Sophia glanced at the countess, wanting to make certain she hadn't heard Dalia's comments. The elderly woman sat in a nearby chair, a cane at her side. Several of her friends visited with her. Hopefully this information wouldn't reach her ears.

"I hope you're not spreading such a rumor," Sophia said at last, unable to keep a note of censure from her tone.

"Of course not. I only heard it a few moments ago and came directly to you."

"From who?"

"Viscount Grover, though I don't believe he meant anyone other than Viscount Rutland to hear." At Sophia's frown, Dalia lifted a shoulder. "I happened to be passing behind them on my way to see my mother. It's interesting what one learns when one is invisible."

"What does that mean?"

Dalia waved her hand in the air. "A topic for another time. But is it true? Is the earl well?"

Aware of Dalia's continued regard, Sophia wasn't certain how to respond. She adored Dalia, but in truth she didn't want to share any information about Elliott. Besides, Sophia knew nothing other than that Elliott had been stabbed.

"Trust you to be unwilling to gossip." Dalia gave a beleaguered sigh. "I suppose it will be one more unconfirmed rumor regarding the earl."

"I suppose so."

Sophia couldn't release her suspicion about the rumors. Were any of them true? Was there a way to discover where and how he spent his days? If she could either confirm or deny his reputation, then perhaps she would know what to do about her feelings for him.

If he was truly a rogue then she had to find a way to harden her heart toward him. Before it was too late. If it wasn't too late already.

"I can see the wheels turning in your mind. Whatever are you thinking?"

"Something I probably shouldn't." And certainly nothing she was willing to share with her cousin.

But now that the idea had taken hold, she couldn't release it. Tomorrow was going to be an enlightening day, one way or another.

※

Late the next morning, Sophia lingered in the hall

upstairs, listening closely for Elliott's departure. She'd overheard him tell Codwell he'd soon be leaving. Guilt for eavesdropping already made her grimace, as had her request to the countess for a few hours to herself to run errands.

What might she feel like by the time she completed her mission this day? But once the idea of following Elliott had come to her, she'd felt certain this was the answer to her dilemma.

There was no harm in her going out.

By herself.

Behind Elliott.

If he caught her, she would simply say— She had no idea what she'd say. She hoped she wouldn't be caught. With a sigh, she smoothed the skirt of the grey gown she'd donned with the hope of blending in.

"Shall we expect you for the evening meal, my lord?" Codwell's voice echoed up the stairs.

Sophia leaned over the bannister, hoping to hear Elliott's reply.

"I suppose not." Was there a note of disappointment in his voice? "I shall see if I can manage it tomorrow evening."

The rest of their brief conversation was muffled, so Sophia retrieved her cloak from her room and rushed down the back stairs. She gave a quick wave at the cook and maids in the kitchen as she passed through and hurried out the back door.

Now if only a hansom cab was waiting down the street, she might be able to follow him. Heart racing, she hurried down the alleyway, clutching her purse. She kept to the alley until she was near the cab stand then ventured onto the street. She nearly cheered with relief when she caught sight of the hansom.

"Will you please follow that carriage?" she breathlessly asked the driver, pointing to Elliott's carriage, still visible in the distance.

"I reckon so," he agreed.

"Don't follow too closely. I would prefer to be discreet." She hopped in and settled on the seat, nerves fluttering.

"Very well then." With a snap of the reins, they were off.

They travelled through the neighborhood, then to Regent Street, where she lost sight of the carriage several times in the snarled traffic. Luckily, the driver's higher perch provided him a better view.

The farther they went, the more Sophia worried that she'd made a terrible mistake with this venture. The risk was too great. If Elliott discovered she was spying on him, everything would be ruined.

At last they drew to a halt along Whitehall near an impressive three-story building. It had to be some sort of government office as all the buildings in this area were. She watched as Elliott alighted and entered.

"What building is that?" she asked the driver.

"The Foreign Office."

Sophia had no idea what to think. What business could Elliott have there?

"What would ye like me to do?"

Sophia pondered her options, indecisiveness filling her. "Would you mind waiting a few minutes?"

Though worried she wouldn't be able to find another hansom when Elliott left, she couldn't afford to pay the driver to wait long.

Thus far, her mission was not a success.

Minutes passed slowly as doubt trickled in, threatening to overwhelm her plan. What had she been thinking? This was an awful idea. Yet she'd already started down this path. She might as well see it through.

As though a reward for her patience, or perhaps her determination, Elliott emerged from the building, striding toward his carriage with a grim expression.

"Shall I follow him again?" The hopeful note in the

driver's voice made Sophia wonder if he was enjoying this game of pursuit.

"Yes, if you please." Sophia settled back into her seat, curious as to where Elliott might be going next. Visiting someone at the Foreign Office was hardly the act of a scoundrel.

It was far too soon to jump to such a conclusion she reminded herself. Yet relief filled her all the same.

In her heart, she didn't want Elliott to be a rogue. While she held little hope they might have a future, she needed to know the truth, before her feelings grew any deeper.

Lost in thought, she glanced out the window, realizing they'd passed into an unfamiliar neighborhood, not that she knew London well. This neighborhood held a worn appearance, as though better days had come and gone.

Grand houses lined the quiet streets but a few of the roofs drooped. Shingles were missing here and there, and many of the wrought iron gates sagged on their hinges like drunken old men propped against a wall.

The cab slowed to a halt and the driver leaned down. "The carriage stopped ahead, and the gentleman is walking toward one of the houses."

Following her instincts, Sophia quickly alighted and handed the driver his fee, all while keeping an eye on Elliott's progress. The chance of him not spotting the hansom seemed slim, and she would soon run out of money. "That will be all."

"Are you certain you don't want me to wait?" The driver frowned between her and the money she'd given him, as though disappointed to end the quest.

Quelling her doubt, Sophia gave a decisive nod. "I will follow on foot from here."

She hurried toward the house where he'd disappeared. Had he gone inside? The squeak of a gate had her walking around the side of the house to follow the sound. She proceeded cautiously, glancing up at the four-story house, wondering who lived here.

Why would Elliott go to the rear entrance? It suggested a familiarity that concerned her. Was this his mistress's home? She bit her lip, hoping she was wrong. She pressed on, more determined to find out what he was doing here.

The murmur of voices reached her from the rear entrance, followed by the sound of the door closing. She continued through the side garden until she could see the empty back step.

Now what? She could hardly knock on the door and inquire as to who lived there.

Or could she? Did she dare do something so bold? Surely, Elliott was no longer anywhere near the door. If an unsuspecting servant answered, perhaps she could pry information from him or her.

Front or back door? Back, she decided, moving before her nerves sent her running. She checked the narrow veil of her hat to make certain it was pulled down, hiding most of her face.

A footman answered the door, at least she thought he was a footman, though he didn't wear a uniform, only a suit coat. "Yes?" he asked.

"I am here to see Mrs. Smith." Sophia looked behind him, hoping to glimpse something that would give her a hint as to who lived here. But all she could see was a bit of the kitchen and the hall, which told her nothing.

"There is no Mrs. Smith here. You have the wrong house." The man stepped to the side, blocking her scrutiny.

"I am certain she told me this address. Who lives here?" Sophia eased to the opposite side, hoping to improve her view.

"You need to leave, madam."

"Are you certain there's no Mrs. Smith?" At the man's nod, she tried again. "Is this a private residence?"

The annoyed servant shut the door in her face.

All the air left her lungs in defeat. What else could she

have said to gain more information? Silly of her to think she might've been allowed to enter. And what would have happened if she had? Looking around the house wouldn't have told her anything. She needed to know who Elliott was meeting with and why.

She walked down the steps and returned to the side garden, glancing at the windows. Unwilling to give up, she eased past a hedge to move closer to the window.

In for a penny, in for a pound.

Heart hammering, she peeked into the room but the glare from the glass hid the interior. She cupped her hand around her eyes. Now, she could see what looked to be a drawing room.

She shifted to get a better view, rising to her toes. Her breath stopped as she caught sight of Elliott. He sat in a wing-back chair, visiting with an attractive woman.

Dropping quickly, she closed her eyes for a moment, praying the woman wasn't his mistress. The idea of him holding the stranger the same way he'd held her had her blinking back tears.

Sophia stayed where she was for a moment, wondering if he'd seen her. She tried to gather her wits and swallow her hurt and determine what to do next.

This had been a terrible mistake. She knew nothing more than when she'd left the house earlier.

Worse, if Elliott had seen her, how could she possibly explain herself?

Elliott stilled, unable to believe his eyes. That couldn't have been Sophia peering in. Not *his* Sophia.

"I fear the news is true," Mrs. Lawrence continued, with Elliott hardly listening. "Two of my girls heard it directly from the Russian diplomats."

"That is alarming indeed." He'd thought that information coming from Mrs. Lawrence would be the worst news he'd receive today.

But he'd been wrong.

The sight of Sophia staring at him through the window was far worse for his heart than the brothel madam's words.

He stared at the window, trying to process how she'd come to be here and why.

He debated whether to continue the conversation with Mrs. Lawrence or pursue Sophia, only to realize there was no debate.

"Is something amiss, my lord?"

"Please accept my apologies. I believe I forgot something." He rose, hoping the woman wouldn't take affront to his abrupt departure.

"Does it have anything to do with the attractive young lady peering in my window?"

Elliott clenched his jaw. Trust Mrs. Lawrence not to let anything slip past her. She ran the brothel like a captain ran a ship, with efficiency and high expectations.

"Yes, it does. I believe she is looking for me."

"Would you like to invite her in?" Mrs. Lawrence raised a brow, an amused smile tilting her lips. "I believe I would enjoy meeting her."

Elliott cursed under his breath. The last thing he wanted was his personal life to collide with his professional one. Though he rather liked Mrs. Lawrence, that didn't mean he wanted her to meet Sophia.

Instead of giving voice to his thoughts, he offered an apologetic smile. "I have no doubt she would enjoy meeting you as well, but perhaps another time."

"I look forward to it."

"Thank you for the information. As always, please send word if you discover additional details."

"Of course."

He rushed out the rear door and through the garden to the window, hoping Sophia hadn't disappeared. Well aware Mrs. Lawrence was no doubt watching, he slowed his steps as he neared the window, but there was no sign of Sophia.

"Sophia?" he called quietly. The random pattern of the tall hedges provided too many hiding places.

A rustle in the foliage just ahead had him moving quicker.

"Sophia."

"Elliott." Her tone held an odd combination of surprise and dismay.

"Were you expecting someone else?" The anger filling him as he found her, crouching by the hedge, took him aback.

"Well, no, but—"

He lifted her to stand before him, grimacing from the pain of his knife wound. A client of the brothel he'd been visiting had gotten angry at his line of questioning. The injury was a physical reminder of the danger in which he was involved.

"What are you doing here?"

"I—I wanted to know where you were going." She lifted her veil, those hazel eyes imploring him to understand. "I spoke to that man at the back door but—"

His angry growl stopped whatever explanation she'd been offering. His heart pounded as his anger grew. The man to whom she referred was one of Mrs. Lawrence's guards. Frank had spent years in prison for murder. Elliott knew of at least three other lives he'd taken since he'd been released. The man was a brute, and Elliott was horrified to think he'd been anywhere near Sophia.

He wanted to shake her for the risk she'd taken. If only she realized she was outside a brothel and had spoken to a murderer. "Why did you follow me?"

Her lips twisted and for a moment, he didn't think she was going to tell him. "I wanted to know where you go every day."

He shook his head and guided her toward the gate. "We are not having this discussion here." The sooner he got Sophia away, the better. Hadn't he known from the beginning that her presence in his home would only cause trouble?

"Whose house is this?" she asked, as she glanced back, tugging her arm, but he held tight.

"No one's." A deep breath did little to calm him.

"Then why were you here?"

They reached his carriage and the driver moved to open the door but Elliott waved him back.

Ignoring Sophia's question, Elliott assisted her inside then leaned against the opening. "Sophia, you cannot follow me ever again. It's too dangerous."

"Dangerous?" Her alarm made him realize his mistake over his word choice too late. "You were involved in a knife fight then tell me you're in danger again. What is happening, Elliott?"

He glanced away before he was tempted to tell her the truth. The only thing that mattered was her safety. His efforts to make her uncomfortable by playing the rogue had failed miserably. But her actions today had proven that he needed her gone, away from him and his terrible, imbalanced life of lies and deceit.

Besides, the man she was coming to care for didn't exist.

"Was that woman your mistress?" Sophia whispered.

He could think of but one way to force her to stay away from him. If only he could explain that this was far more painful for him than for her.

"Yes," he said as he braced himself. "That was Mrs. Lawrence, and she's my mistress. She knows more about pleasing a man than you will ever learn."

He gritted his teeth and his belly burned with disgust for his lie, but he couldn't think of any other way to keep Sophia away from him.

Tears filled her eyes as she stared at him.

"I don't understand what you think our relationship is, Miss Markham," he continued. "You are my grandmother's companion and have no business following me around London. I don't appreciate it."

The stunned hurt in her expression squeezed his heart, yet what else could he do? If she followed him again, she might be injured, or worse, killed, and he'd never forgive himself.

"I'll inform my grandmother that you've decided to seek another position at a home more suitable to you." He forced himself to offer a cold smile. "You've known from the start who I am. Wishing doesn't change a scoundrel to a gentleman. Nor do a few kisses."

Her tiny gasp made him want to take away her pain with a kiss, tell her how sorry he was, and that he wished things could be different. She'd captured his heart and he didn't know how he would survive from this moment forward.

"Surely you didn't think you and I would ever suit." He shook his head, as though amused at the idea.

Still, Sophia said nothing.

"You need to be gone by the end of the week." He shut the carriage door and nodded to the driver to go. As he watched it turn the corner and disappear from sight, a coldness filled him, making him wonder if he'd ever be warm again.

Though he knew he'd done the right thing, it didn't make it easier. Nor did he know how he was going to survive without Sophia in his life.

Chapter Ten

Sophia's tears didn't stop until the carriage arrived home. Elliott had a mistress. He didn't want her.

"Surely you didn't think you and I would ever suit." The terrible words rang through her mind, over and over.

She never should've followed him. As she'd feared, her actions had ruined everything. She'd lost any chance with him. She'd lost her position. She'd lost the countess.

She'd lost her new life.

Never mind that, as Elliott pointed out, there had never been any hope for them. She'd just been too naïve to realize it.

Oh, heavens. What was she to do now?

By the time the carriage drew to a halt and the footman opened the door, Sophia had collected herself. The last thing she wanted was to create a scene in front of the servants. Instead, she focused on her anger at Elliott for having a mistress while he'd been kissing her.

That anger propelled her up the stairs to her room. But hurt quickly returned as anger slipped away. She looked around her room, tears filling her eyes at the thought of leaving.

Tonight, she and the countess were attending a concert. They were in the middle of planning the party. How could she possibly leave?

The Elliott who'd said such hurtful things was a new side of the man she'd grown to care for. Or rather, to love. His harsh words hadn't changed her feelings. She'd fallen in love with a scoundrel despite all her efforts to the contrary.

Unfortunately, he didn't feel the same. The truth of that seeped into her bones, making her ache. As she sank onto her bed, wiping tears from her cheeks, his comments returned to haunt her. Those words had been her worst fears come to life. The voice of Aunt Margaret echoed through her thoughts, recriminating her for following in her mother's footsteps.

Odd how it had only been after she'd asked if the woman was his mistress that his demeanor had changed. What if she hadn't asked that question? Would he have explained the danger he'd mentioned? How had the conversation turned so quickly to him telling her they didn't suit and she had to leave?

Once again, an encounter with Elliott left her bewildered and reeling. His words stabbed straight to her heart.

Drawing a shaky breath, she attempted to calm herself. She needed to check on the countess. Soon they'd be preparing for the evening, and the countess was looking forward to the concert.

Sophia refused to mention anything about Elliott dismissing her. He could deliver the news himself.

Her own actions were the only things in her control at this moment. She rose and rinsed her face, hoping to erase the outward signs of her upset. She was determined to make the most of her last few days here, and that started with the concert this evening. She might never have another chance to attend one, certainly not with the countess.

She planted a smile on her face despite the tightness of her cheeks. Then she lifted her chin and walked to the countess's room, hoping she could make this evening special for both of them.

⨯

Weary to the bone, Elliott entered Prime Minister Gladstone's waiting area in the Foreign Office building as late afternoon eased to twilight. The rest of his day had been spent checking with as many sources as he could with the hope of discovering where and when the violence Mrs. Lawrence had confirmed would occur.

The *who* part of the equation had been identified. Dmitry Popov, a Russian anarchist Elliott had met in Paris, was at the heart of the plan. He was a music critic and composer, but of late his political interests had taken precedence over his career.

Popov was determined to make a statement that would capture the attention of not only the Queen and London, but also the world. That meant a prominent building or event, possibly with hundreds of people in attendance.

Yet how could they stop the plan if they didn't have any further details?

Despite the urgency of the situation and such high stakes, the image of the anguish on Sophia's face as he'd shut the carriage door gripped his thoughts and refused to let go.

She'd left him no choice other than to force her from his life. Her personal safety mattered far more than either of their feelings. While he knew he'd done the right thing, that didn't make it any easier. He ached with the loss.

Viscount Rutland rose to greet him. "Aberland. I thought I'd join you for your briefing with the Prime Minister."

"Excellent." Elliott appreciated the man's presence, especially given his own distraction.

Though Rutland spent most of his time in the office and had little field experience, his sharp mind and instincts made his input helpful.

"Perhaps you can assist in making sense of all this," Elliott said.

"It is a puzzle, isn't it? The Russian anarchists have done a good job of providing false leads to cause confusion."

"We have to determine the facts soon, else we will be too late." Impatience burned in Elliott. He was certain an attack of some sort was imminent. Beyond that, little had been confirmed.

"The prime minister will see you now," Mr. Lyttelton, Gladstone's private secretary and nephew, announced as he held open the door for the men.

Gladstone rose from behind his desk to greet them, his lips drawn, a sure sign of his concern. With thinning white hair, sparse mutton chops, and a solemn demeanor, he was an intimidating man.

"My lords," he said as he nodded. "I hope you come with news. The Queen is as anxious as I am for a report."

His poor relationship with the Queen was well known. Elliott didn't envy his position of delivering more bad news.

"Yes and no," Elliott replied. "Dmitry Popov is planning the attack, but the target and timing remain elusive. Most clues indicate something in the next day or two."

"My sources point to Popov as well," Rutland agreed. "I have taken the liberty of putting together a list of events that should draw significant crowds in the next two days with the hope we can cross reference it with the information gathered and narrow the options." Rutland withdrew a piece of paper from his breast pocket and spread it on Gladstone's desk.

After several minutes of sharing what each had learned and comparing that to the list, the target soon became clear to Elliott.

"The Royal Albert Hall." His heart sank. "Popov is a

composer and made it clear he thinks the hall is an atrocity." The very place his grandmother and Sophia were going this evening.

"Surely he isn't planning something for the concert being held in a few hours?" Rutland appeared horrified at the thought.

"I think that is exactly what he's doing." Elliott's chest was so tight he could hardly breathe.

"That gives us little time," Gladstone said.

Rutland shook his head. "Destroying the concert hall when it has only been open a few weeks would be a blow not only to London but to the Queen personally."

"Precisely why he would choose it," Elliott added. "Hundreds of people, perhaps even thousands, will be in attendance." His gaze met Gladstone's then Rutland's. "Including my grandmother and her companion."

Gladstone pulled his watch from his vest pocket. "Let us hope we can find a way to stop the attack. I will send word to as many men as I can to aid you."

"My carriage is outside." Elliott was already striding toward the door. Despite his efforts to keep his loved ones safe by keeping his position a secret, they were in more danger than he could've imagined. His heart raced, his limbs felt heavy, and a thick fog clouded his brain.

"What will we be looking for?" Rutland asked, directly behind him.

Elliott drew a deep breath, trying to gather his thoughts. Now more than ever, he needed to think and act clearly, but at the moment doing so felt impossible. "My guess would be some type of explosive. Popov has experience with them and it would injure many as well as destroy the concert hall."

They were soon riding through the crowded streets in Elliott's carriage toward the hall.

"Where would be the logical spot to place the explosives?" Rutland leaned forward, his gaze holding Elliott's.

His practical questions shifted Elliott's focus from panic and worry to the task at hand.

The best way for him to protect his grandmother and Sophia was to stop the attack. As impossible as it seemed, he needed to try to set aside his personal fears for their safety and shift his efforts toward halting the terrible plan. Lives were at stake.

"Perhaps under the hall, where the foundation is." But the hall was a large place. Even with the assistance of the other men who were supposed to join them for the search, chances were slim they would actually locate the explosive, especially since they didn't know what they were looking for.

"We will find it. Have no worries," Rutland said, as though sensing his concern. "Your grandmother and her companion will not even realize something was amiss."

Elliott nodded, appreciating the confident words even if he didn't believe them.

"The hall was built over Gore House," Rutland said. "I'm certain you remember Her Majesty laying the foundation stone. That would've been in May of 1867."

"That's it," Elliott declared. "What better statement than to put the explosive near the very stone the Queen placed herself?"

"Brilliant. If memory serves, that is under Stalls K, Row 11."

Rutland's wealth of information might just save the day. "That is where we shall check first."

Night fell in full as they crossed the city toward the hall in South Kensington. Elliott prayed they would arrive in time and find a way to stop this madness.

※

Sophia alighted from the carriage behind the countess at The Royal Albert Hall. They had enjoyed a delightful dinner at the Chatfield's, and she was looking forward to the concert. Apparently, they weren't the only ones as the street was filled with traffic.

She smoothed the skirt of her pale yellow gown, one of the new ones the countess had insisted she have. Sophia had never been overly concerned with fashion, but she liked the cut and color of this one. The matching cloak fit snuggly over the bustle and the fastener was a flower fashioned out of the fabric. The maid had swept her hair into a high chignon but left one long ringlet to trail over her shoulder.

She knew she looked her best, but she felt brittle, as though she might shatter at any moment. It had taken incredible effort to smile and act normal with the countess as they moved through the evening, and it was long from over. Enjoying the events was impossible for Sophia, but she didn't want to ruin it for the countess. Her only hope was to focus on the moment and not think of tomorrow or the day after.

"Very striking." She studied the round domed building made of red brick with torches lighting the entrance.

"Isn't it, though? I have heard there is a terrible echo inside," the countess whispered, as they made their way up the steps toward the entrance amidst the large crowd. "Can you imagine how disappointed the Queen must have been when she heard that?"

"How unfortunate, especially for a concert hall."

"They have placed a decorative canvas awning in the roof in an attempt to improve the acoustics." The countess pointed to the ceiling where the canvas was clearly visible.

"Does it solve the problem?"

"I understand it helps. The lighting is impressive. A special system was installed in the hall that lights over a thousand gas jets in less than ten seconds."

Sophia murmured appreciatively as the countess shared other details.

Three levels of seating inside the rounded interior allowed everyone attending to both hear the concert and have an excellent view.

They slowly made their way toward their seats. Luckily, the countess had her cane to assist her. This much standing and walking would no doubt tire her.

Dalia and her sister, Letitia, her husband and two other couples were already seated. They exchanged greetings as they took their seats.

Sophia had never attended an event like this. She enjoyed music, and, despite the sadness that weighted her heart, anticipation filled her as the musicians took their place on stage in the center of the hall.

"Oh, dear." The countess glanced around her seat and the floor. "I seem to have dropped my fan. I had it when we entered the hall."

"I will look for it," Sophia said, rising.

"I'll accompany you," Viscount Frost, one of Lettie's friends offered. "I need a breath of fresh air."

His wife, Lady Julia, smiled. "Don't be overlong, else you'll miss the opening performance."

Dalia had mentioned to Sophia that the viscount didn't care for crowds. No doubt he welcomed the excuse to escape for a few moments.

"Thank you," Sophia said as they walked up the aisle, already searching for the missing fan.

"My pleasure," the handsome viscount offered. His gaze swept the floor as well.

The crowd had thinned considerably with most people having taken their seats. They neared the entrance before Sophia spotted the familiar fan. She bent to retrieve it when someone caught her eye.

Rising slowly, she studied the man who lingered near the entrance. He shifted as though unsettled or anxious, tugging at his cravat as if it choked him.

"Do you know him?" the viscount asked as he stepped nearer.

"No."

"He doesn't act as though he's here to enjoy the

music."

Before Sophia could reply, the man stiffened, eyes wide as his attention caught on something. She followed his gaze, her heart pounding at the sight of Elliott and Viscount Rutland rushing into the hall. The pair headed directly toward an interior door, their urgency noticeable even from this distance.

"Isn't that Aberland?" Frost asked. "Where are he and Rutland going?"

"I'm not certain, but that man is following them, and he appears very unhappy at their arrival." Another man followed as well. Without a second thought, Sophia hurried after them, certain the danger Elliott had mentioned was directly behind him.

※

Nothing Elliott did slowed the heavy pounding of his heart. All he could think about was his grandmother and Sophia somewhere inside the concert hall. His worry made it difficult to think, to focus.

The last thing they needed was a panicked crowd. Requesting well over a thousand people to leave the hall in an orderly and expedient manner would take time they didn't have. The other men Gladstone had sent for would have to help with the evacuation.

Luckily, Rutland had been to the hall before. "There's an access door here," he directed, opening it to reveal a set of stairs.

Several lanterns waited at the top, no doubt left for maintenance purposes. Elliott lit one before they hurried down.

The music rumbled below the stage as the musicians warmed up, vibrating the stone foundation. Elliott felt that vibration to his toes, the sensation worsening his simmering nerves.

"This way," Rutland said. "Stalls K are just there."

Within moments, Rutland navigated to that section of the foundation. Massive columns supported the structure. Rutland stopped abruptly before the red granite stone the Queen had laid with a golden trowel nearly four years prior.

A dusty wooden box sat on the floor beside the column. Elliott nearly passed by, only to stop and stare. Dusty and dented, it looked like something a worker had inadvertently left behind, but it caught Elliott's notice.

He knelt beside it, noting recent fingerprints smudged the dust. A quick examination revealed the dust was actually talcum powder. "This could be what we're looking for."

The box was approximately two feet by two feet and about a foot tall. Big enough to contain explosives. He tried to lift the lid but to no avail.

"Locked?" Rutland knelt beside Elliott.

"I believe so, but I don't see a latch."

"This side is hinged. The opening must be on the other side," Rutland said.

Elliott lowered to the ground so he was at eye level with the lid. He pulled a knife from his boot and slid it carefully along the crack. A little wiggling of the blade provided a satisfying click.

He held Rutland's gaze for a long moment then returned his attention to the lid. "Are you ready?"

Rutland licked his lips. "As ready as I will ever be. Is field work always this nerve-wracking?"

"Rarely." Elliott returned his knife to its sheath then used both hands to slowly raise the lid. He released the breath he hadn't realized he held when nothing happened.

A tattered piece of canvas hid the contents. Moving slowly, Elliott lifted the cloth. He had only seen explosives one other time, in Paris. This one was similar. The sticks of dynamite were wired to a small clock. The relentless ticking was audible even over the music being played above them.

"I'm guessing that when the alarm rings, the fuse will light, causing the dynamite to explode," Elliott said.

"They must expect these casks of liquid paraffin to explode as well."

Elliott glanced over his shoulder to where Rutland stood next to several wooden casks of the fuel. "Then we had better make certain we diffuse this. More barrels may be placed throughout the building."

"Halt."

The deep voice with its distinct accent caught Elliott's attention. A man stepped out of the shadows into the lantern light. The pistol he held caused Elliott's mouth to go dry. "Popov. Surprised to see we've discovered your ridiculous plan?"

"Not so ridiculous when there is nothing but rubble standing in place of this despicable hall."

Another man joined Popov, bigger and broader, with a nasty grin on his face.

Elliott glanced at Rutland, hoping the man knew how to fight. From the surprise on the viscount's face, he hadn't expected this.

Movement in the shadows behind the Russians drew Elliott's gaze. The face he briefly glimpsed before the darkness hid her set his heart racing.

Sophia.

No. Not after the sacrifice he'd made. The idea of her and his grandmother nearby had been difficult enough. But to see her in the middle of this terrible situation was unbearable.

If anything happened to her...

He swallowed back the thought. He refused to allow that, especially not when he'd ended things between them so badly, hurt her so terribly.

More than anything in this world, he realized how much he wanted the chance to tell her he loved her.

Chapter Eleven

Sophia watched from the shadows with her heart in her throat as the anxious man, his cohort beside him, pointed a pistol at Elliott.

She didn't pretend to understand what was happening, what these men wanted, or what Elliott and Rutland were doing down here. She only knew the gun could end Elliott's life.

Elliott slowly stood when she wanted to scream at him to take cover. She knew he'd seen her and was no doubt angry with her for following him once again. In this moment, she didn't care, nor did she care that he didn't have any feelings for her. She only wanted him out of danger.

But how?

Frost bent close from where he stood behind her, his whisper barely audible. "I'll take the one with the pistol. You distract the other."

Distract? Her mind went blank at the request. Perhaps that was for the best. If she thought this through, she'd be paralyzed by fear.

That would never do. Not with Elliott's life at risk.

She stepped forward and looped her arm around the

second man's arm, taking him by surprise. "Lovely hall, isn't it?"

The large man stared at her in surprise then struggled to free his arm, but she held tight and stomped on his foot.

Her efforts were small but provided the distraction Frost requested. Frost hit Popov's hand before he could react to her presence, knocking the pistol to the ground, then struck Popov in the stomach. Elliott rushed forward to drive his fist into the larger man's jaw, and Sophia shifted out of the way.

Rutland scrambled forward to retrieve the gun, while Elliott pinned the other man to the floor.

Sophia's breath stopped as she saw the contents of the box beside the column. "What on earth?"

"You'll never determine how to stop it," Popov declared as he struggled to extract himself from Frost's tight grip.

"What's going on down here?"

Sophia spun to see Captain Hawke, Lettie's husband, enter the circle of light.

"When you took so long to return, I came to see if something was amiss. Apparently, I was right." Hawke raised a brow at Elliott.

"You could say that. Can you three take charge of these men so I can try to diffuse the explosive?" He rose as he spoke, leaving the large man in Hawke's capable hands. He squeezed Sophia's hand as he passed by before kneeling before the box.

Sophia stared in shock at this new side of Elliott. Would she ever know him in full? She didn't understand what was happening, or how he had the knowledge or skills to deal with any part of the situation.

"You cannot stop this." Popov chuckled, an unpleasant sound that sent shivers down Sophia's back.

"If I remember correctly from the explosive you left in Paris, the trick is to disengage the fuse."

Popov sobered as Elliott pulled out his knife once

again. The intensity of his expression as he worked had Sophia watching closely, holding her breath. The tension in the room made the music playing above sound harsh and grating.

At last, Elliott sat back on his heels, returned his knife to its hiding place, and dusted off his hands. "That should do it."

Everyone in the room breathed a sigh of relief, except for the two strangers. At Rutland's direction, he, Frost, and Hawke escorted the criminals upstairs. One of Elliott's associates came and retrieved the box, removing it from the building for safety, leaving Elliott and Sophia alone for a moment.

As the swell of the music above quieted, Sophia braced herself, filled with uncertainty now that she and Elliott were alone. His expression told her nothing.

"I'm sorry I followed you again when you told me never to do so. But when I saw that terrible man follow you down here, I had no choice."

He didn't reply, only gathered her in his arms and held tight, as though he'd never let her go. She didn't know what to think, what to feel. Tears filled her eyes as the warmth of his embrace sank in. She hugged him as well, grateful for the moment.

He eased back, the emotion in the depths of his glittering jade green eyes making her breath catch. "I'm the one who needs to apologize. I'm sorry for the terrible things I said to you. They were all lies. I have no mistress. I didn't mean any of it. Pushing you out of my life was the only way I could think of to keep you safe."

Relief filled Sophia at his words. "None of it was true?" As what he said sank in, hope sparked deep inside her.

"I only said those things to protect you, to force you out of my life. After everything you saw this evening, I realize I can no longer hide the truth from you. I would ask that you hold this in confidence. Keeping my secret is the only way I know to protect those for whom I care."

Though a hundred questions came to mind, she held her silence, waiting, holding tight to the idea that he cared for her.

"My position with British Intelligence has taken enough of my life. I intend to give my resignation to Prime Minister Gladstone before the week's end."

Sophia frowned. "Intelligence." Her mind reeled with the information. "Does that mean you are not truly a..." She hated to say it.

"Scoundrel?" He laughed as he drew a finger along the ringlet trailing over her shoulder, causing her to shiver. "Much of my reputation served as a cover for my work."

"Much but not all." Sophia smiled, her heart singing.

Elliott sobered, his gaze dropping to her lips. "Sophia, this is a terrible time and place but I cannot wait a moment longer." He took her gloved hands in his and met her gaze. "I love you. I will never let you go, not ever again."

The sweet declaration had Sophia blinking back tears once again. "I love you, too, Elliott. More than I can say. More than I ever imagined possible."

⁕

Elliott waited in the foyer of his home, pacing the small area as impatience burned within him.

Ten days had passed since the terrible night at the concert hall. Ten long days as Sophia had went to stay with the Fairchilds at Elliott's insistence so he might court her properly. He'd advised the prime minister he would no longer be working for the Intelligence Office. Gladstone had attempted to change his mind, but Elliott remained firm.

He had a new focus now, and it didn't involve playing the rogue or gathering intelligence. While he felt he walked on shaky ground without either of those identities, he was determined to forge a new path with Sophia at his side.

His grandmother was delighted at the change in

circumstances and insisted that had been her plan all along after meeting Sophia. She'd had no doubt that her new "companion" would be the perfect match for Elliott.

Like any good grandson, he'd thanked her for her meddling from the bottom of his heart.

Guests would arrive any minute for the party Sophia and his grandmother had spent so much time planning. The countess insisted Sophia dress for the event here, in case any last minute preparations were needed.

Elliott hoped for a moment alone with Sophia, but if she and her grandmother didn't come down soon, that moment would be lost.

As he turned to pace in the opposite direction, movement from above caught his eye.

His breath whooshed from his lungs at the sight of Sophia descending the stairs. The pale rose silk gown fit her perfectly, emphasizing her slim curves. A trail of pearls swirled along the front, echoed by a pearl pin in her dark curls.

Her hazel eyes caught his and didn't let go until she placed her gloved hand in his.

"Sophia. You are beautiful."

She smiled. "I feel like a princess this evening. When your grandmother selected this gown for me, I thought it too ornate, but she was right. I love it." Her gaze swept over his black and white attire. "You look so elegant."

He bowed over her hand then drew her close. "I wanted a moment alone with you. Before the guests arrive."

"Oh?"

Steeling his nerves had become an easy task over the years, but tonight, he couldn't push them back. His stomach trembled with them, he couldn't catch his breath, and the words he needed eluded him.

All because of the woman before him.

With his heart in his throat, he went down on one knee. "Sophia, will you do me the honor of becoming my wife?"

She gasped in response, eyes wide as she stared at him in shocked delight. Her beautiful eyes glittered with tears as joy lit her face. "Elliott!"

He rose, her hand still in his as he kissed her long and deep in an attempt to show her just how much she meant to him.

Then he eased back to look into her eyes. "I don't think you've answered," he said, his nerves threatening to return.

"Yes! Oh, yes. I love you more than I can say." She tugged her hand free to lift on her toes and wrap her arms around his neck, kissing him until his passion urged him to take her back upstairs.

"Well now," the countess interrupted as she descended toward them. "I assume this means someone has something to tell me?"

Elliott shared a smile with Sophia before reaching for his grandmother's hand. "Indeed, we do. Sophia has just agreed to become my wife."

"That is excellent news." His grandmother beamed at both of them. "Especially since this is an engagement party. I feared I had the timing wrong after all. Wait until you see the cake Cook baked to celebrate."

Elliott shook his head at her. "You are incorrigible."

"I do believe your grandfather said that once or twice as well." She gave Sophia a hug. "Welcome to the family, my dear. I couldn't be more pleased."

"Nor I, my lady." Sophia smiled brightly.

"And you, dear boy." She gently pushed Elliott's chest. "I thought you were never going to open your eyes and realize the treasure standing before you."

"My apologies for taking so long to come to my senses." Elliott chuckled.

"The pair of you may have another minute or two, but I expect you both in the receiving line shortly to greet our guests. I'm going to check the ballroom one last time to be certain all is as it should be."

Elliott wasted no time drawing Sophia into his embrace for another kiss. "I love you, Sophia. I don't know how I've lived this long without you."

"I never realized tempting a scoundrel would be quite so exciting. I just needed to tempt the right one."

"I cannot wait to show you how exciting it will be." With a smile, Elliott kissed her once again, his heart full now that Sophia was in his arms forever and always.

The End

OTHER BOOKS BY THE AUTHOR

Victorian Romances:
The Seven Curses of London:
Trusting the Wolfe, a Novella, Book .5
Loving the Hawke, Book I
Charming the Scholar, Book II
Rescuing the Earl, Book III
Dancing Under the Mistletoe, a Novella, Book IV
Tempting the Scoundrel, Book V
Falling for the Viscount, Book VI, Coming Fall 2017

The Secret Trilogy
Unraveling Secrets, Book I
Passionate Secrets, Book II
Shattered Secrets, Book III

Medieval Romances:

Falling For a Knight Series:
A Knight's Christmas Wish, a Novella, Book .5
A Knight's Quest, Book 1
A Knight's Temptation, Book 2, Coming Nov. 2017

The Vengeance Trilogy:
A Vow To Keep, Book I
A Knight's Kiss, Book 1.5
Trust In Me, Book II
Believe In Me, Book III

If you'd like to know when a new book is released, I invite you to sign up to my newsletter to find out when the next one is released: http://www.lanawilliams.net

If you enjoyed this story, please consider writing a review!

ACKNOWLEDGMENTS

This book wouldn't have been written without my talented critique partners, Michelle Major, Lani Joramo, and Robin Nolet. I'm so grateful for your help on this journey! My beta readers are brilliant as well and include Linda Benning and Tracy Emro. Your feedback helps more than I can say!

Reviews help authors tremendously and also help other readers find books, so please consider leaving a review. They are much appreciated, and I read them all.

More historical romances are coming your way!

Made in United States
Orlando, FL
20 June 2023